Cerulean

A Novel

A. L. Singer

Cover art by Tham Nguyen Design.

Acknowledgments

To my many siblings, thank you for all your support and encouragement.

To my father, who always teased me about my never-ending stories, and to Connie, who is anything but my "other mother"—I love you both and know you are proud.

To my husband, whom I love and adore. With you beside me, I was able to get through my darkest days and look forward to tomorrow.

To all my prereaders—Natalie, Kim, Gina, Ferin, Adam, Laura, Angela—thank you for your opinions and feedback. I'm glad you all loved the book and repeatedly told me to get it into the world.

To my editor, Lisa Drucker, thank you for all your help, hard work, and encouragement.

I turned back to the graveyard once more before getting into the car. The rain had started to intensify from a light mist to heavy drops. The pings echoed on the umbrella someone held over me. A hundred yards away, I looked one more time at the canopy over the two caskets covered with white roses. I just stood there, numb, not wanting to walk away. Twenty-three was too young to be burying my parents. The air was thick and hot, and the rain only made it worse. I swallowed hard, in spite of the lump in my throat, and whispered good-bye.

"Mia. ... Sweetheart, it's time to go." I barely heard my name when Jennifer's husband Aaron spoke it. I closed my eyes, releasing the tears that filled them. Finally turning back to the car, I slid into it. Someone closed the door for me. I lay my head back on the seat and closed my eyes. My fingers played with the pearls around my neck. I had borrowed them the week before from my mother's jewelry box. Visions of her wearing them filled my mind. The car started to move slowly, swaying over the gravel beneath us toward the main road. I would be home shortly.

I drifted off and recalled the day I died inside. Ever since the phone call a few days earlier, I had felt empty within. I had been up in the attic finishing a series of paintings for the local deli. As I concentrated on the holes in a block of Swiss cheese, the phone rang. Seeing the name flash across the screen, I thought it a little odd my mother's best friend was calling. Odder still, from her cell phone. I assumed she was going to scold me for not coming with my parents to her annual Fourth of July celebration. Only before I could finish the word hello, I heard her crying.

My blood ran cold. "Jennifer ... what's wrong?" I heard myself say. A part of me instantly knew it was bad. Just five years before, my boyfriend, Gavin, had drowned during spring break. His mother had called to inform me. Sorrow was all I had heard in Gavin's mom's voice too. Jennifer's crying brought me back to that heartbreaking time.

Jennifer's voice cracked on the phone. "Gina saw everything ... she was headed home. She left the same time as your parents." More crying, but I couldn't ask anything. All I could do was listen as she continued. "They were the first through the intersection when the light turned green. Mia ... the other car ran their red."

I dropped my paintbrush and crumpled to the floor, unable to sit on my stool. Jennifer's voice started to sound far away, and the room began to tilt. "Poor Gina was only two cars behind them." She sucked in a sharp breath. "Mia ... Mia, honey, they rushed your mother to the hospital. I've sent Aaron over to get you and meet us at the hospital." She started sobbing "Mia ... you there? Do you understand everything I just said?"

I realized I had yet to respond to what she was telling me. I couldn't move; I was frozen in disbelief. This was not real. Glancing to the small window on the opposite side of the attic, I saw that it was just after dark outside. Jennifer's voice was back, only she was speaking to someone else. "I don't know," I heard her say. She started crying again. "She hasn't said a word yet. …" Then her voice came through the phone louder. "Mia, please answer me."

I took a deep breath and spoke into the phone, my voice a monotone. "My mother and father were in an accident on the way home from the barbecue. They rushed my mom to the hospital. Dad is fine, and Aaron is on his way here to take me to the hospital." I said it so matter-of-factly, as if I were reporting the weather. I somehow picked myself up off the floor and started down the stairs to the second floor. Jennifer starting sobbing again. "Mia, I am so sorry. I didn't. … The accident was really violent. The other driver was speeding, and when he hit your parents' car, it threw them into a pole." She choked trying to catch her breath. "Your dad is not fine. They didn't rush him to the hospital … because they couldn't do anything for him. The paramedics said it was probably … he didn't feel any pain, Mia." She cried louder. "He was already gone by the time the ambulance arrived. They were lucky to get your mother out of the car so quickly. …" Jennifer's voice trailed off.

I grabbed the banister as my knees went weak. I only made it down a few steps before I collapsed on the stairs below me. "Mia, I'm at the hospital now. I have to hang up. I'll see you soon." The phone went dead, and I simply let go of it. It bounced down the stairs and landed a yard or so in front of the inside of the front door.

Just then there was a frantic knock at the door, and then Aaron burst in. He kicked the phone unintentionally as he rushed in looking for me. I couldn't move toward him; I couldn't move, period. My whole body felt so heavy, and I was unable to lift it from the steps. My dad was gone … just like that—gone.

"Mia, we have to go now!" Aaron rushed up the stairs to me, putting his arm around my waist. He got me to my feet and walked me down to the doorway, bending to retrieve a pair of sandals lying near the entrance. I couldn't even find my voice to say they were my mother's, not mine. He fumbled as he tried to help me into them, and then he shut the door behind us.

The car ride to the hospital was similar to the current one home from the cemetery. A hazy blur in slow motion, with the same disbelief running through me. I'm sure Aaron sped that day to the hospital. He knew the severity of the situation and wanted to get me to my mother. Even if it was only to say good-bye to her. Be there for her last moments alive.

But it was too late. I knew it as soon as the ER entrance door opened in front of me. Jennifer and her twin sister, Gina, were rocking back and forth, sobbing with their arms wrapped around one another. Aaron caught me before I collapsed. I closed my eyes as the realization of it all began to sink in. I was all alone; no mother and no father. The hospital could have been empty for all I cared. I had never felt so utterly abandoned and alone before that moment. In a blink of an eye they were taken from me forever. The tears started, and all I could do was softly whisper no, over and over again. …

The car came to a halt in the present, and someone squeezed my hand tenderly. "Mia, you're home, honey." Jennifer's voice cracked a little, and she started to cry. I opened my eyes and stared at the ceiling of the car. This wasn't my home anymore. Nobody I loved with my whole heart waited inside for me. The house had become an empty shell just as I had.

I sat up and looked toward Jennifer. Even with tear-streaked cheeks she was beautiful. She had shoulder-length blonde hair that was currently pulled into a bun at the base of her neck. She wore a black cotton dress with a sweetheart neckline. My eyes lowered briefly as I fought my own tears, unable to see hers.

Jennifer also wore a small silver snowflake pendant around her neck. I couldn't remember the significance of it, but I knew it was a gift from my mother years ago. Her hand left mine as she moved to wipe away her tears. I looked up to see that Jennifer's sapphire eyes had shadows under them. She cleared her throat and smoothed her dress. I didn't want to go inside the house I used to call "home." Now it was a place that would constantly remind me of my pain and loss.

Aaron left the driver's seat and stepped back to open Jennifer's door for her. She stepped out and her husband shut both car doors. He wrapped one arm around his wife, holding an umbrella in his other hand. Aaron leaned forward and whispered something into her ear. Some kind of encouragement I was sure; yet another reminder of what I had lost. I remembered my parents hugging every day. My father always whispered some encouragement after my mother had a difficult day.

I turned away and reached to open my car door. It opened before I lifted the handle, the rain had returned to a heavy mist and it drifted into the car. It tickled my face as I looked up and saw Kayla, Jennifer and Aaron's daughter. She looked just like her mother, only a younger version. She was newly eighteen and normally the most upbeat girl you would ever meet. Kayla glanced back at the house before speaking. "There are a lot of people inside already, Mia." Her voice was so soft, and concern slowly washed over her face. I was exhausted, mentally and physically. I wanted the day to be over. I didn't want to be around people another minute. I yearned to be alone, to curl into a ball and convince myself it was all a dream. Kayla's forehead wrinkled a little more. She saw it on my face, the dread of going inside and hearing the condolences over and over. Hearing stories and reliving the memories of my parents throughout the house. I glanced at the front door, at the people pouring in, and swallowed hard, barely getting past the knot in my throat.

Aaron led his wife to the front steps, kissing her temple just outside the door as he shook his umbrella free of the rain. "I'll sneak you in the patio door if you want. I'm sure the mama bears will take care of everything Mia." Kayla forced a smile that didn't reach her bright-blue eyes. The "mama bears" were what Kayla and I called our mothers and her aunt Gina. The three women were partners in the town's coffee shop with attached bakery. Of course now there were only two mama bears.

"No, I can do this Kayla ... but thanks. You have done so much the past few days. I just want to thank you." I finally climbed out of the back seat, stood up, and hugged her. Giving her a quick squeeze, I headed into the house.

My eyes traced it as I slowly walked. A two-story cream-colored house with large front windows facing the road. I avoided looking at the attic windows so I wouldn't think about where I'd been when the awful call from Jennifer came. Rosebushes lined the path to the front door. It was at the end of a cul-de-sac, and cars were now overflowing the circle. I passed the front door as it crowded with people shaking off their umbrellas before entering. I made my way to the side of the house and entered through the garage door. Once inside I continued through the mud room to the large kitchen and looked around. Friends and coworkers of my parents along with my only family member present filled the kitchen.

My uncle Massimo—my dad's brother—had come in from out of state and, thankfully, took care of my parents' arrangements. He had lost his only sibling, who was only a few years older than he. He saw me and made his way across the room. The past few days had been rather awkward. I had not seen him in over two years; he'd lived on the other side of the country for as long I could remember. Our families rarely got together. Massimo and his wife were West Coast, and we were East. "How are you doing, Mia?" He was genuine in his concern. "Your mother's friends have coffees and teas from the shop. They also brought a selection of baked goods from the bakery. I'll go get you something to eat … you look a little pale." He was almost pleading with me to eat. I wasn't hungry. I couldn't even force myself to eat. Gently shaking my head no, I began staring off into space, and he gave up, leaving my side.

Jennifer was at my side all of a sudden. "When did you eat last?" I tilted my head to the left and looked past her. My eyes met my uncle's, and he quickly looked away. I hadn't watched him but knew he had run to a mama bear when I turned down something to eat. She asked me again and then began rambling. I realized that I was a distraction for her, if only for a minute. Someone to fuss over and keep her mind occupied.

"No mama bear today …" I said. "Please, Jennifer, don't fuss over me." I tried to sound grateful for her concern but feared I'd hurt her feelings anyway. I knew I wasn't the only one who lost loved ones, not the only one grieving today. But they were my parents, not anyone else's. Jennifer looked down and slowly turned away. I took a few steps away myself, standing in the doorway between the kitchen and the dining room. I couldn't go through the dining room to the family room where everyone else was. Couldn't share memories and listen to stories.

Jennifer must have recovered from any hurt feelings I had caused because she held a plate of fruit and was walking in my direction. I quickly looked for Kayla, flashing her a look of desperation for help. She called for her mother just as Jennifer reached me, something about being out of sugar. The mama bear turned and motioned to Kayla she would be right there. She held out the plate in front of me. I did the only thing I could to guarantee a moment to myself. I forced a smile and took the plate from her. Jennifer left my side after patting my back and giving me a quick kiss on the cheek. "I'll let you be for the day, Mia … or at least the next few hours." She was stern and I knew she meant it.

"How about a week without you hovering over me, mama bear?" I tried to smile. I wanted to walk right through the doorway on the opposite side of the kitchen. Down the hallway to the guest room where I had stayed since the accident days ago, only having a few hours of sleep here and there. The lack of sleep was catching up with me. Crossing a room seemed too much at the moment. There were so many people at the island filled with pastries and coffee, I couldn't possibly make it past everyone without being stopped. I turned again to the family room and noticed a few people at the bottom of the staircase.

The one thing about my house that struck others as odd was how different the upstairs and main level were from one another. Down here on the first floor it was picturesque, something you would see in a home style magazine. The kitchen was filled with the newest appliances. A marble-topped island with copper pots and pans hanging above it sat a few feet from the sink and counters. Dried herbs hung from the cherrywood cupboards and always scented the room. The dining room had a few pieces of artwork hanging on the walls. There was a dining room table where we actually sat as a family and ate meals together whenever we could. I looked at the huge oak table with chairs that were too heavy for me to move as a child. The family room was through the opposite doorway across from where I stood now. I could see the beautiful stone fireplace with a few small sculptures on the mantel. Again just a few pieces of art hung on the walls.

I could just see the bottom few steps to the second floor from where I stood. I didn't look farther up the stairs. I began to wonder how many more days would pass before I would ascend that staircase and look at what waited to surround me once again. As beautiful and simple as the downstairs was, another world greeted you at the top of the steps. I sighed, trying to block it from my mind but failing miserably. Upstairs the walls were covered in family pictures and my childhood artwork. Endless frames captured every possible milestone of mine. A close-up of my almost-year-old smiling face, with my first tooth visible. Another held a picture of me with melted chocolate ice cream all over my face and a soggy cone in my little hand. I had always assumed that because I was an only child, my parents had wanted to capture and display things like my first ice-cream cone. The artwork that hung above the doorways upstairs was nothing foreign or bought from galleries like the downstairs. My name in crayon claimed artistry randomly throughout the pictures. Then somewhere in my mother's feminine print would be something like "Mia's first tree," "Mia's tiger after a trip to zoo," and so on.

Upstairs was my bedroom—the one I had known my whole life. With walls that had seen many colors of paint over the years. Windows that had been covered in everything from a pink nursery print to my favorite cartoon character. But my bedroom wasn't the only one upstairs. My parents' room was above those steps also. Their room that held their bed and pillows that I ran to when it stormed as a child. I would bury myself in between them and pretend to be scared just to be near them. I would enjoy the smell of their pillows around me. I'm sure those pillows upstairs still held their scent. My father's of mint; my mother's, floral, usually rose. *No!* I wanted to stay downstairs away from a gallery of pictures that displayed a family that no longer existed. And bedrooms that held bittersweet memories. I wanted to escape to the guest room down the hall through the kitchen.

Maybe if I kept my head down and didn't make eye contact, everyone would let me pass. No one could fault me for wanting to be alone, maybe even hide until everyone left. I pictured crawling into my temporary bed, pulling the covers over my head. All alone, no parents on either side of me. I was surprised when my eyes started to water and a few tears fell. I honestly didn't think I had any left to cry.

"Mia?" I heard my name and blinked. "Mia, you're standing in the same spot I left you thirty minutes ago. And all the food is still on your plate." I was taken aback when Jennifer took my elbow and led me into the dining room. I started to shake my head no. I didn't want to move from the safe spot I had found. *You promised!* I screamed in my head. She took my plate and pulled a chair from the table. I froze; I hadn't seen them. Pictures ... more than a dozen of them, framed and laid out, covering most of the table's surface. It was a wave of pain straight through my heart. My parents smiling up at me from our family portraits. My head started to spin, or maybe it was the room. I hadn't eaten a real meal in days and was operating on a few hours of sleep in the past seventy-two hours. To now see my mother and father who were forever lost was enough to make me completely shut down.

Everything went into slow motion. I turned away from the table, away from the pictures. I tried to move, but my legs weren't responding. I grabbed at the back of one of the chairs as my legs turned to mush. All of a sudden, the few people in the foyer were rushing to me. Everyone was reaching for me and saying my name with panic in their voices. I let go of the chair and was falling down, my eyes fluttered as I saw the ceiling above me. Everything went black as my body hit the floor.

Chapter 2

I could hear voices that sounded like they were in a tunnel some distance away. One voice said, "Oh … Aaron! … Aaron, I think she passed out. I told her to eat something. I should have made her eat." That would be mama bear Jennifer hovering over me. Then I heard other voices, muffled, off in the darkness surrounding me. "Is she all right?" one voice asked. "Should we call for help?" another wanted to know.

Then I heard his voice, crystal clear. An accent, Romanian possibly. "There is no need for that," he said. "Mia … Mia, open your eyes for me." His voice was soft and warm.

My body tingled, and I wanted to obey. My eyes fluttered, and I saw light for a second before they closed again. A part of me refused to rejoin the world around me. *No,* I thought. *I just want to lay here in the darkness; let me be.* There was a light caress on the curve of my neck. It wasn't until then that I realized my head hadn't hit the floor like the rest of my body. My head shifted slightly, but I had not moved. I felt someone touch my face, sensing it was the stranger with the warm soft voice. His thumb traced my cheek, and I knew my head was resting in his hands.

He spoke again in that same voice, at once tender and alluring. "Where should I take her?" There was heavy silence for a minute, followed by Jennifer's fumbled answer. "Um … follow me." And with that I was floating through the air. My eyes fluttered again in the kitchen, and I saw familiar dried herb bouquets and a flash of copper. I smelled sandalwood and felt soft fabric against the side of my face.

Soon I was in the guest room, sinking into the bed. A hand gently ran down my arm and rested over my palm. A few muffled voices again. I could not make out the words but heard slight panic and concern. *Leave me alone.* I thought. *Just go away.*" I wanted to scream. *Leave me here in my darkness. ... Alone.*

He spoke again trying to reassure mama bear. "She will be fine, Jennifer. ...I will watch over her; she just needs some rest. Go make sure the guests are attended to. I will call on you as soon as she wakes up." His voice was heaven, soft and soothing.

Jennifer answered with a low and empty whisper. "You-will-call-on-me-when-she-wakes." I heard the soft movement of her leaving the room and the door closing behind her. I began to stir. She left me—just like that. No fussing. No hovering over me. The stranger had called her by her full name, I realized suddenly. Only her closest friends and family called her Jennifer. Even customers at the coffee shop called her Jenny. I called her both. Whatever mood she was in on any particular day determined whether I called her Jenny or Jennifer. Since the accident, though, I had only called her Jennifer. Whoever this stranger might be, Jennifer must know him.

He slid his hand around my ankle now, lifting it an inch or two above the bed, just enough to slip off my black high heel, and then he did the same with my other foot. The sensation of tiny bubbles climbed my spine. A blanket drifted over my body, covering most of my legs and some of my abdomen. I could feel his presence. He stood at my side or maybe over me. Suddenly his breath was at my ear. "Sleep, Mia. ... Sleep and know I will not leave your side."

A beautiful promise. I sighed. Such a chivalrous promise from such a beautiful voice. But it meant nothing to me. If I had the strength I would have told him to leave. Everyone I truly loved had left me. Absurdly enough, this stranger thought his words would mean something to me ... on this day. My head fell to the side in his direction, and just before I fully embraced the depths of sleep my eyes opened slightly. They were so heavy, this movement took all I had. A tingle spread throughout my body, and my heart felt absent briefly. I caught a glimpse of him. He was angelic looking, with perfect pale skin. Ice-blue eyes, a strong jaw line with a touch of stubble. His shiny black hair was combed back from his face except for a few loose strands that fell over his forehead. He looked a little past thirty, and I knew I had never laid eyes on him before now. I fantasized that maybe he was my angel, here to take me to my parents. To end the pain that filled me. It was what I wanted in that moment. My eyes drifted to his lips, pale pink and full. *Take me ... my beautiful angel, from this awful place. Make the pain cease. Please.*

The words failed to leave my mouth as I tried to reach out to him. He took my hand as we just looked at each other, quiet and still in that moment. My eyes moistened when I understood how foolish my fantasy was. He looked toward the door and then leaned closer. "Sleep, Mia." My eyes grew heavy and I did as he said. I had no strength to fight sleep anymore.

Soon I was sitting on a dock surrounded by water lilies. The air was fresh and crisp, as if it had rained earlier in the day. All the lilies were fully opened and snow white, framed by the bright green pads around them. I eagerly wanted to touch one, hold it in my hand. I reached out to pick one but jerked my hand back when my father's voice boomed. "No, Mia!" he yelled frantically. I spun my head to look over my shoulder. There he was on the opposite side of the dock lunging forward. "Mia!" he exclaimed. "You really scare daddy some days. If you want a flower, you just need to ask." He wasn't looking at me; he wasn't even speaking to me. He reached down and plucked a lily from the water. My father turned to his right with it facing away from me. I turned my body around to watch him. A tiny voice spoke up. "Thank you, daddy … it's pretty." There I was at his side, only four or five years old. Big black curls framing my face. Bright eyed with rosy cheeks. …

I was dreaming. I had this dream at least once a year. The only recurring dream I ever had. It was actually one of my first childhood memories. The dream was always the same: me beside my dad on a dock surrounded by water lilies. Little Mia almost falling into the water trying to reach a flower. This time the mood was different. I didn't want to watch, didn't want to relive this memory. My father reached over and pinched my cheek. "You need to be more careful, okay?" His voice loving and stern. I wanted to look away. My heart began to ache. My father wasn't real; he was not really here only a few yards away from me. I tucked my knees up against my body and rested my chin on them. I wrapped my arms around my legs and started to rock my body slightly. "Wake up, Mia, wake up." I started to cry, repeating the same words over and over. I rocked my body harder and clenched my fists. "Wake up now!"

I cried out and jolted up in bed. My eyes, still filled with tears, tried to adjust to the dimly lit room. Without warning, strong arms embraced me and held me tight. "*Shh …* It is all right now." He whispered, holding me against him. "Just a bad dream."

My body lost some of its tension. "Bad dream." I repeated. Yes it was all a horrible dream—the phone call, the accident, all of it. My dad must have heard me crying and come to wake me up. He was still here, and my mother was probably in the kitchen cooking something for breakfast. I inhaled deeply, trying to smell something sweet. Waffles with syrup or cinnamon rolls … anything comforting. But nothing sweet filled my nose. Instead it was a woodsy aroma, sandalwood or cedar.

My eyes shot open. I instantly knew. This wasn't my father holding me so close, trying to comfort me. I shoved the soft-voiced stranger away, moving backward until my body was pressed against the headboard. I couldn't speak, only stare at him and let it all sink again. I looked down at my dress in the dim light, felt the string of pearls around my neck. It *had* all happened. Earlier in the day I had left my parents in the cemetery, now surrounded by other lost loved ones. They were gravestones to visit and bring flowers to. More tears filled my eyes, and I just let them fall down my cheek.

He reached for me, but I shrank away. His ice-blue eyes looked right through me, and he let his hand fall to his side. "Do you want me to retrieve Jennifer for you, Mia?" He said it slowly, shifting his body to go. Glancing at the door and then turning back to me. His eyes searched my face, waiting for a response. A vague ache filled my body. I remembered falling earlier in the dining room and then hearing his soothing voice. He had carried me to bed and tucked me in. There was a chair next to the bed. The pretty white wood matched the vanity across the room. As soon as my eyes fell on the chair, he stood up from the bed and sat on it.

I realized hours had passed; there wasn't much light coming in from above the curtains. I looked at the clock on the vanity to confirm, squinting as I tried to focus. He reached over to the nightstand next to him and passed me a glass of water. I wiped away my tears and took it. I drank half the glass and set it back on the table. The stranger just sat there, watching me in silence. I thought he was an angel before. Here to take me away to a peaceful place without pain and sorrow. But he didn't; I was still here. If he wasn't my angel, who was he? Why had he sat here this whole time? I didn't feel threatened; eerily, I felt just the opposite. Actually not feeling uncomfortable about his presence alarmed me a little inside.

He tilted his head slightly and shifted in the chair. He wore a navy-blue sweater, a lightweight knit, but a sweater in the heat we had been experiencing was odd to me. I cleared my throat and finally spoke. "You could introduce yourself. Jennifer may know you … and you obviously know my name, but I know that you and I have never met." It came out as a demand and rather rude. But I didn't care. He was in my house and in my room.

He stiffened, sitting up straight in the chair. "I apologize. I should have introduced myself as soon as you awoke, Mia." He shook his head, and his eyes fell to the side of the bed. "I only came for you ... I mean stayed here with you to make sure you recovered ... after that fall." His voice was consistently soft and gentle, as if he thought speaking to me like this would make the moment less awkward. "Sorin. My name is Sorin." He held out his hand for me to shake. But I just looked at it and pulled the blanket draped over me a little higher.

"You knew my parents?" I asked. His ice-blue eyes met mine, and I shivered. Every time he looked at me directly, my stomach knotted up a little. He never just "looked at me"—no, he saw into me somehow. I felt vulnerable, exposed in some way.

"I knew your mother, Evelynn, but I never met your father, Mia." His accent was thicker on some words. The way he said my name, as if he knew me personally, really annoyed me.

"She never mentioned a Sorin, and you don't sound like you are from around here," I countered.

His gaze fell away. "I met your mother many years ago when passing through town once."

It sounded like a single meeting many years ago. My parents were wonderful people. My mother was the sweetest woman you could meet. My father, Vincent, was an architect, mostly for hotels. Both had crossed paths with many people in their lifetimes. But everyone I had seen today I had known or at least heard of. Why come a distance for someone you met once? I felt confused and suspicious. "You met her years ago, and now you've come all this way to pay your respects. Have you been in touch with her this whole time?"

He looked at me but quickly turned away, mumbling something. Sorin's jaw flexed tight. He was silent a moment, and then he spoke slowly. "Your mother was a very brave, very strong woman. I may have only had a brief encounter with her, but it forever altered me."

I shuddered when he fell silent again. He had meant every word. He'd actually seemed a little uneasy as he said the words aloud. I was about to ask more but heard voices in the kitchen. The clock said it was late evening. I sank down into the bed and sighed. "Are there still a lot of people here?"

Sorin looked at me and then glanced at the door. He tilted his head and seemed to think for a moment. "Not many; six or seven guests are still here. Close friends of your mother." He said it so matter-of-factly. "Do you want me to get someone, or would you prefer that I walk you out?"

I knew I should go back out there, at least to let the mama bears know I was all right. I considered it some more. I didn't want to leave this room; it had slowly grown darker, and I wanted to stay right here forever. Sorin took my silence as an answer and leaned back into the chair. "Are you feeling a little better now that you rested?"

I contemplated the simple question, as the answer was anything but. My head was still reeling in disbelief from the events of the past few days. My heart literally ached, filled with utter pain, whenever I focused on what had happened. But for the first time in days my body felt like some stress had left it. My eyes weren't burning from lack of sleep and never-ending tears either. "Yes, actually I do, physically." I answered at last, surprising myself.

Looking to the doorway, I heard the voices again. I rubbed my temple and whispered to myself, "I wish they would leave. I can't do this." I wanted today to be over. I looked at Sorin and felt conflicted. I didn't know him. My mother had never mentioned him, but I felt like there was something more than what he'd told me. He spoke of my mother with an admiration that was touching. I wanted to continue talking to him. For the first time in days the conversation wasn't about me surviving this experience, and his eyes weren't filled with pity. As peculiar as this whole scenario was, a part of me didn't want it to end. I shifted my body, preparing to leave the bed finally. "I'm going to freshen up and then join everyone. Will you stay a little longer?" It came out as a plea, and I winced. It must have sounded desperate.

"I will stay as long as you want, Mia." Every time he spoke, Sorin's words and voice seeped into me. I started to slide my legs over the edge of the bed to stand up. Sorin quickly stood and moved the chair he had been sitting on out of my way. I just sat on the edge of the bed for a minute. When I was sure I was able to stand I crossed the room to the bathroom. I felt his eyes on me as I passed him. Just before entering the bathroom doorway, I turned back to thank him for his kindness. But the guest room door was closing its last few inches.

I turned on the bathroom light and stood in front of the mirror. I looked awful, and I moaned in disgust. My long black hair that had been smoothed back in a low ponytail was now loose and wild. I leaned in closer. My mascara had become black smudges under my eyes. My eyes themselves looked grayer today than their usual mix of colors. I gave up years ago trying to decide what color they were. They weren't dark in any way, just a combination of gray, green, and some light brown. If I wore green they seemed to follow. My optometrist laughed about not being able to figure it out himself, telling me to put hazel on my driver's license. I looked pale and drained, and my stomach growled. I couldn't remember the last thing I'd eaten. Resting my palm over my abdomen, it felt hollow, empty. It matched my heart.

      I heard a few low voices somewhere down the hall. I stepped out of the bathroom and looked at the guest room door. I stood still, waiting for Jennifer or Gina to walk through it. To my surprise, minutes passed, and I relaxed again. I went to the love seat off in the corner of the room. A pile of my clothes lay covering the cushion. They were the only clothes that had been on the first floor, still in the washer. I had washed them the morning of the accident, forgetting about them once I started to paint—I left clothes in the washer like that pretty often. And then the accident happened, and nothing else mattered. I was now wearing the same clothes over and over. A pair of jeans, three shirts, two pairs of socks, and some undergarments. I just washed them again when needed. I couldn't bring myself to go upstairs and get more clothes. Thankfully, nobody seemed to notice, and I was too embarrassed to ask someone to retrieve some clothes for me from upstairs. I was sure if Jennifer or Gina knew I was struggling so much in my own house they would have insisted that I go home with one of them. I had sent Kayla up for the black dress and heels I wore today. She hadn't questioned the request, much to my relief.

After staring down at the pile of clothes, I just lifted a pair of dark-washed jeans and a dark-green V-neck T-shirt. I locked the guest room door before taking off my mother's pearl necklace. I laid it on a silver tray that had been my grandmother's many years before. My fingers ran over the pearls. I unzipped my dress and was shrugging out of it when I felt a slight soreness in my lower arm. I let the dress fall to the floor and returned to the bathroom lighting for a closer look. Just above the underside of my left wrist, I could see two small bruises. I tried to recall bumping into something or hurting myself recently. The fact that they were almost perfect circles struck me as strange. I passed my fingers over the bruises again; they were tender but not painful. Stopping my fingers right on top of them it all made sense. They were left from someone's fingers earlier when I passed out. Whoever had tried to catch me before I hit the floor wasn't worried about being gentle at the time; it was a good thing I hadn't broken my neck or gotten a concussion.

I looked at my reflection. At five foot, six inches and 130 pounds, I was average height and weight, with a few Italian curves to my body. I hadn't been down to the gym room in our basement for many days now, even though I still looked toned. I had lost some weight from not eating lately, and I didn't care. I didn't want food and couldn't imagine eating. I looked at my loose wavy hair, which had lost the perfect curls of my childhood. It fell to the middle of my back when I didn't pull it back. I washed my face clean, redid my ponytail, and then shut off the bathroom light. I pulled on my jeans and T-shirt in the dark of the guest room, as there was hardly any light coming in from above the curtain. Rain faintly fell outside. I took a deep breath and prepared myself for the fussing and scolding for not taking care of myself.

Chapter 3

Slowly walking down the hall to the kitchen, I listened for the voices I'd heard before. But I heard none now. As I reached the kitchen I just stood there. Was everyone gone? No fussing, no scolding, or pity-filled eyes. I wondered if they were just quietly sitting in the other room. Sorin cleared his throat as he entered the opposite doorway. "Is everyone in the other room?" I asked, hoping it wasn't true.

"No. ...Everyone has left." He paused and tilted his head slightly. A few wrinkles appeared on his forehead. "It is what you wanted, is it not, Mia?" he asked.

It was what I wanted—all that I wanted—to be alone. To just climb into bed down the hall and never leave it. I shrugged and crossed to the island filled with fruit and pastries from the coffee shop and bakery my mother used to help run. I looked up at Sorin as he moved to join me. "Yes, it is what I wanted ... to be alone."

He stopped and turned back to the doorway. "I will leave you then." He sounded hurt or betrayed, or maybe both. It caught me by surprise. I hadn't wanted him to leave; I just didn't want the mama bears fussing over me. I wanted to ask him to talk some more about my mother. Hear something that she had never told me. Plus, the thought of being truly alone for the first time in days made me shudder. The past few days people had come and gone, called nonstop. My uncle had even taken the upstairs guest room the last few nights. I was relieved when I saw him pack before leaving for the funeral home. Someone had always been in the house with me. But now that I'd actually left my parents in the cemetery, it had come to an end. No more food being dropped off, no more friends of my parents stopping by to say how sorry they were. No more waiting to see them one last time to say good-bye. My father's casket was closed because of the head trauma. I could have seen my mother's face one more time. Dying of internal bleeding made an open casket viewing possible. I had been told she looked beautiful. But I couldn't bring myself to go to see her for myself. After days of waiting to see them, I hadn't. Setting white roses on each of their caskets at the burial and whispering good-bye was all I could do. I wanted my last images of them to be when they were alive and happy.

Now I felt like nothingness was slowly claiming me. No one to rush down to in the kitchen to wish a good morning. No one to talk about the day's events with over supper. I wanted my parents back. The pictures of my mother and father were too much. Their room ... the smell of my mother's pillow would have absolutely killed me in this moment. But hearing about her from a stranger with a foreign accent didn't seem overwhelming. A part of me wanted that.

"Sorin, I asked you to stay, and you said you would." My voice fell a little and I looked down. "Please stay and talk to me for a little while." *All alone,* I thought to myself, *sooner or later you will be completely and truly alone.*

"Mia, I will stay if that is what you want." He crossed the kitchen and pulled out a stool. He sat on the other side of the island across from where I stood. Between us there was food, teacups, silverware, and tins of tea in different flavors. He relaxed on his stool and just watched me. The silence continued, beginning to feel a little awkward. Looking at the disarray between us, I was amazed that the mama bears had left such a mess. There was a short note in Jenny's handwriting saying to call if I needed anything.

"Would you like some tea and a scone, or coffee and something?" I asked, doing something to occupy myself, keep busy. Sorin glanced over everything laid out between us. "I will have the same as you," he said after a moment.

Looking down at the food, I knew I should eat, but I had lost any desire for food. "Oh … I'm not hungry. But I'll get you my favorite tea and a croissant." I tried to sound pleasant. Quickly turning to get him a plate and napkin, I poured some hot water from a teapot that was left on the stove and placed the cup in front of him. After picking the largest croissant, I plated it and was laying it on the counter in front of him when my stomach rumbled. Sorin caught me by the wrist suddenly, and I froze. I looked up at his eyes, ice blue and invading. His grasp was firm but gentle. I wasn't scared or threatened, but I twisted my wrist in effort to free it all the same. "Sorin?" I simply said his name as a question. He didn't release his grip.

"Mia, you should eat something." His voice was caring, genuine.

"Really, I'm not hungry." I whispered and tried turning my wrist away again. Looking down at his hand wrapped around my wrist, I noticed it was not far above the small bruises. It was quite possible he had been the one who'd left them while coming to my aid earlier. My eyes darted back up to his, and he blinked, quickly letting go.

I watched his lips tighten briefly. "I apologize, I did not mean to. ..." His voice trailed off. A few lines reappeared on his brow. Sorin placed his hands on top of his legs and relaxed his shoulders. I started to clean up the marble counter between us. When he spoke again, his voice was extra soft, alluring and soothing. The way it had sounded when I blacked out. "Mia ... look at me," he said slowly. My eyes felt heavy suddenly as they met his. "You fainted earlier today ... yes?" He nodded his head a little.

I slowly blinked and nodded my head. "Yes, I fainted," I whispered. My head felt light, and my body went lax.

He continued "You probably have not eaten in days." His angelic voice flowed over me.

"I have not eaten," I confessed.

Sorin's eyes held mine as he paused before speaking again. "You may not want to eat, but you must. Eat something ... please." His tone was firm and his accent more prominent when he spoke like this to me.

I felt as if I was about to faint for the second time today. My body slowly grew heavier. I blinked again slowly and sidestepped to a stool, sitting down. Sorin finally broke his gaze, pushing the tea and plate toward me. Without hesitation I picked up the croissant. My head started to clear, and my stomach rumbled. No longer ignoring what my body needed, I sat there and ate. Slowly tearing apart the croissant and eating it piece by piece. I sipped the tea as Sorin sat quietly, just watching me.

I finished the tea and went back to the stove, hoping the water was still hot. I poured some into my cup and returned to my stool. He had placed another croissant on my plate. I imagine the face a child would make at the supper table when told to eat more broccoli crossed mine. I sighed and looked across the island at him.

His eyes softened, and his voice purred, "One more." He pushed the plate a little closer to me. I frowned but ate it piece by piece, as I'd eaten the one before. Again Sorin just sat and watched. I would glance up at him every time I sipped my tea. When I finished, I pushed the plate down the counter and out of his reach, making it clear I was done eating. I felt more myself. My body no longer had a fuzzy feeling. I glared at him. "There. I ate. Happy?"

His eyes softened again, and the corner of his mouth turned up just a hint. It wasn't a smile, just a look of triumph he was trying to downplay. "I am very pleased, actually." There was a touch of arrogance in his voice.

"My mother," I blurted abruptly. "You said you knew her, or at least had this life-altering encounter with her." I was only repeating what he had said previously. He straightened his shoulders and glanced around the room, avoiding my eyes. "You said you met her, my mother." My heart fell. Had he lied or exaggerated in some way? "Did you lie?" I accused him.

Sorin's eyes turned from some invisible spot on the wall and locked with mine. They were wide, and he leaned toward me. "I did not lie to you, Mia. I promise." A pause. "I would not lie about knowing your mother." I had just met him, but a part of me knew he was telling the truth. I relaxed and closed my eyes, taking a deep breath. "Then tell me how you met her and why you speak about her with such regard."

When I opened my eyes, his face was blank, vacant. "I have never shared it with anyone. It was a day that forever changed me, and yet I have never spoken of it." Sorin was so serious, so somber.

I slowly shook my head. "You sound as if she saved your life or something."

He was silent a minute or two. "Actually, it was the opposite." He winced. I could see him recalling everything. "I saved hers."

I gasped in disbelief. "What?!" My mother never said anything about a near-death experience or anything close to it. Confused, I asked, "When did this happen?" My tone was demanding.

"Twenty-four years ago … minus two months," he said and then stopped.

"Go on. What happened? Tell me everything," I pleaded as my heart started pounding in anticipation.

Sorin slowly stood up and started to back away from the counter. His eyes were fixed on me, but I could see his mind racing. He shook his head. "I am truly sorry, Mia. I believe a terrible mistake has been made in my coming to you. … In this time of grief, I do not want to upset you further."

I felt his words held something deeper. I jumped from my stool and raced to his side as he walked away. "Don't go," I begged. My eyes started to water; I was on the verge of crying. "You didn't make a mistake." I looked down at the floor, fighting the tears. "You won't upset me."

I started to look at him. Sorin's hands were fists at his sides. I was suddenly desperate for him to stay and tell me what happened. I stepped closer to him and covered his fists with my hands. They were cool and unmoving. My gaze lifted from our hands to his face. His jaw flexed, and he pressed his lips tightly together. I was almost afraid to meet his eyes. Sorin's whole body read hostile and tense. I didn't know if he was upset about talking about his encounter with my mother or if I had done something wrong. Sighing, I lifted my eyes the last few inches to his. My heart ached a little; his eyes weren't frightening at all. They seemed panicked or scared. I spoke in a whisper. "Sorin, you didn't make a mistake coming here." His arms relaxed a bit. "You won't upset me." His hands eased enough for me to budge them from his sides. I felt a tear fall down my cheek. His eyes went from panicked to saddened, and his jaw lost its tension. Not sure I had convinced him to stay and tell me everything, a few more tears fell. I looked back at the floor, repeating my words one more time. "You didn't make a mistake … stay … please." My voice cracked.

His hands slowly opened and intertwined with mine. "I will stay if it is what you want. But let me say what I can about that night and no questions after." I didn't totally understand his request. I felt like most of what he said meant something more. Maybe I just did not understand his side of it all. Sorin had saved my mother's life years ago, and now she was gone. It was an experience neither had shared with anyone else. I was frustrated but would have agreed to anything in that moment. Eventually, I became very aware of him softly holding my hands. Feeling strange about the contact not bothering me, I blamed it on all the hugs, squeezes, and hand patting over the past few days. I had no personal space anymore.

Twisting my hands free, I wiped my cheeks dry. "I'll do my best," I said in a forced voice and went back to where I was sitting before.

Sorin took his seat across from me and began telling me what he could. "It was one of the first warm nights of the year in this region. I was out walking around. … I was going to meet up with a friend." He paused, and I took a sip of my tea, vaguely noticing a slight bitter taste this time. I didn't pay much attention to that, focusing all my attention on Sorin. Looking over my shoulder, he was remembering the night he met my mother, moment by moment. He continued, "I heard a scream at the end of an alley I was passing. …"

His eyes shifted and locked onto another place in the kitchen. "I promise you, Mia … I came to her aid quickly … but it was too late." I froze, waiting for him to continue. My chest tightened, and I started to feel nauseated.

Sorin resumed his tale. "I believe your mother and Jennifer were closing up for the night. Taking the trash out to the Dumpster in the alley behind their shop." I knew exactly where he meant, and from then on I could picture everything he described. "There was a man over your mother as she lay on the ground, fighting for an envelope—money from the day's receipts, I assume. Jennifer lay in the doorway, a bag of trash at her feet. She was hurt and unconscious." He had saved her too. It explained why Jenny was comfortable with my being alone with him today.

Sorin's back stiffened, and he looked down at a spot on the counter between us. "There was so much blood …

your mother's ... it was slowly staining her white blouse. He had stabbed her, Mia, for whatever money was in the envelope." The corner of his mouth twitched. "The man ran off as I approached. I called for help and applied pressure until medical assistance arrived. They rushed your mother and Jennifer to the hospital."

My mouth filled with saliva, inexplicably, and my stomach did a few flips. But it was the bitter taste in my mouth that made me push my teacup away. The image of my mother lying bloody and helpless brought tears to my eyes.

Sorin was quiet. He looked up at me and shook his head. "I did not mean to upset you, Mia. I tried not to go into too much detail in order to spare you."

My mother had never said anything about being attacked, robbed, or stabbed. It must have been such a traumatic experience that she didn't want to relive it. It certainly explained how close my mother and Jennifer were. Going through something like that together bonded people. I wiped my tears away and took a deep breath. "Thank you," I said quietly, my voice unsteady. I took another deep breath. "Thank you for helping them and doing what you could. Caring about two women you had never meet before. I'm sure my mother could've bled out right there. Not many people would have risked getting involved in a situation where their own life could have been threatened." I sat not sure what else to say.

I stood up and started to clear away the rest of the food. Looking back at Sorin, I remembered he had given me his tea and croissant. "I'm sorry. You must be hungry or at least thirsty. I'll get you something." Placing a muffin, a scone, and some fruit on a large plate, I passed it across the counter to him.

"Thank you," was all he said as he took it from me.

"Would you like coffee or tea?" I asked over my shoulder as I rummaged for plastic bags and containers for the food. "What do you recommend?" Sorin asked.

I just shrugged. "Anything but the mint tea blend I just had." I turned to see him looking at my cup. I nodded toward it. "It left a horrible aftertaste. Weird. It never did that before."

His eyebrows rose just a bit, and he looked up at me and then back toward the cup. Slowly standing up and taking a step back, he said, "It has become late, and you have had a long day. I should go now." His voice was odd, forced.

"Do you have to go?" I asked, hoping he would say no and stay longer. I was sure there was more to his saving Jennifer and my mother. He had to have talked to my mother while waiting for an ambulance. Saw that she made it to the hospital. Maybe even visited her while she recovered. I thought maybe if he stayed a little longer and felt more comfortable he would share more. It was pretty late, and I couldn't imagine he actually had some where to be. Then it occurred to me he hadn't actually said where he was from. The accent, the way he was overdressed for the current heat wave.

"You're not from around here, right?" It was really a statement, but I said it as a question. "Do you need to catch a flight in the morning or be somewhere soon?" I just stared and waited for his response.

"No, where I call home is pretty far from here … and I have no prior engagements currently. I traveled quite a distance for you … for your mother's service, I mean. Maybe you could suggest a place for the night, though."

His accent was hypnotic at times. There was a very nice hotel not far away that my father had designed himself. I stood thinking of what I wanted to say. All I knew about Sorin was that he had saved my mother's life years ago. He had come to my aid today when I fainted. He seemed kind and caring. Something about him comforted me. I was an emotional mess currently, which didn't seem to bother him. A part of me worried that if he went to a hotel I might never see him again. Not hear all the things I felt he was withholding. The house did have a second guest room upstairs. My uncle had returned home, leaving it unoccupied.

"You don't need to stay at a hotel," I said at last. "There is a guest room." I stumbled over my words. "I mean, I'm staying in the downstairs guest room … but there is a second one upstairs." I gestured to the two different directions as I spoke. I could see him thinking, contemplating what to do.

Sorin bowed his head. "You really have been kind. I am sorry for the pain and loss you are experiencing. But I should be on my way now."

His words were so heartfelt and genuine. I couldn't risk the possibility of never seeing him again. I didn't want to be completely alone just yet, and he was a mysterious distraction for me. "You are going to stay here tonight, and I won't take no for an answer." I tried to sound confident. Striking a pose and lifting my chin.

Sorin's face softened, and his lips formed a half smile. He reached up and ran his fingers through his hair. "How could I say no to you, Mia?" He didn't sound completely comfortable with accepting my offer. He slipped out the front door and quickly returned with a black suitcase, leaving it in the doorway between the kitchen and dining room.

I finished clearing the rest of the countertop. Sorin sat down again. I could feel him watching me as I moved around the kitchen. I should have felt uneasy, but a calmness had come over me when he agreed to stay. "Sorin, tell me about yourself. Where are you from?" I yawned. "What do you do for a living?" I asked as I placed the last container in the refrigerator and turned to look at him for a response. Only as I turned around, he was right there. Slamming into him, I jumped. "Oh, I'm sorry! I didn't mean to ... I just thought you were still ..." I motioned toward his previous location, taking a step back from him.

"I did not mean to startle you, Mia." He spoke soft and low. Which was appropriate, considering how close we were standing to each other. My heart skipped a beat. Feeling rattled, I took a deep breath to relax. The smell of him filled my nose—the same sandalwood aroma as before. My head started to feel light again, and I swayed. His hands were suddenly around my waist to stabilize me. I leaned forward and rested my forehead on his chest, closing my eyes.

"Are you feeling all right?" he asked. "Should I walk you to your room?" Sorin's hands tightened around my waist. I didn't want to retire for the night. More nightmares awaited me. I had trouble fighting the dizzy feeling in my head. All I could think about was how intoxicating his scent and voice were. I hadn't stood this close to an attractive man in a few years. Maybe I'd just stopped noticing them.

"No … I'm just … a little … I want to keep talking," I finally managed. I felt Sorin's body tense and then relax. He leaned forward, his cheek brushing mine. His lips were just an inch or two from my ear. "Mia," he purred. "Take a couple of deep breaths for me." I obeyed. My head didn't clear any, though; it only worsened. I swayed against his hands, and my knees became weak. His arms fully embraced me, and he spoke again in that voice. The one that I swore seeped into me. And I loved it.

"Mia, it is late and you are obviously drained. Which is to be expected. Allow me to walk you to bed."

No! I thought. *I want to know more about the night you saved my mother.* A part of me wanted to learn more about Sorin too. "But I want to talk more," I softly complained.

"I promise we will talk more … but only if you promise to tell me all about yourself."

No, I thought again. But I said, "If that's what you want." It was a whisper against his chest. I screamed in my head, mad at myself. I had thought one thing but agreed to another.

"To bed you go," he breathed into my ear just before scooping me up and carrying me to the guest room down the hall. I melted into his arms. All too quickly he gently set me on the bed, resting my head against the pillows and draping the blanket over me.

Chapter 4

The light flicked on before Sorin walked out the guest room door. "I will return momentarily with some more food for you. Maybe it will silence your stomach." His voice had lightened; he sounded faintly amused.

Sorin left the room, and as if on cue, I could feel the rumbling. I rested a hand on my stomach until its complaint was no longer heard. My head slowly cleared, and I was only slightly groggy by the time Sorin returned with a plate of food and a glass of juice. He sat the glass on the nightstand next to me and then placed the plate on my lap as I sat up. I moaned and let my head fall back against the headboard, causing a loud thud.

I looked up at him standing over me. His eyes narrowed, shifting to the plate and then to my eyes. I started to move the plate away from me but stopped when Sorin cleared his throat and took a few steps toward the door. He halted at the foot of my bed, looking down at the plate and then back at me. He made his intention clear: no food, no Sorin.

I glared at him momentarily, only to give in right after. The plate had a muffin, a scone, and a bunch of fruit on it. The same plate of food I'd given him earlier. I picked up the muffin. After a few bites, I looked back up at him and then toward the white chair not far from the bed. Sorin didn't move. I raised the muffin to my mouth but paused, raising my eyebrows at him. He pulled the chair closer to the bed and sat down. I finished the muffin and a few pieces of fruit, and I drank some juice. Sorin took the plate from my lap and set it beside the glass on the nightstand. I watched him relax back against the chair, his mood improved.

"Now tell me about yourself, Mia." He crossed his arms and waited. I wasn't one for sharing details about myself. I didn't really have any close friends and was not social. I fidgeted a little, not sure where to begin. What was I supposed to say? A vision of myself in an interrogation room with a bright light above me filled my mind. I rolled my eyes at him. "What do you want to know?" I fussed. "Ask." My voice expressed my frustration, and I crossed my arms tight against my chest.

"Everything," he said simply.

I stayed silent, wondering why I had agreed to talk about myself.

"Occupation," he finally suggested.

I took a deep breath and cleared my mind. "I make most of my money from paintings I do during the week. My mother hangs a lot of my artwork in the coffee shop to sell." I felt that familiar ache in my chest. I corrected myself. "My mother used to sell my artwork in her shop." I continued trying to suppress the negative thoughts starting to rise. "If you go into any doctor's office or bank in town, my artwork will be on the walls." I wasn't being conceited; it was a fact. "That's the way this town is. We all support each other. Buy from one another if we can." I took another sip of juice. "But on the weekends I work as a bartender on the other side of town. For Leo, a friend of my parents." Sorin raised an eyebrow at this for some reason. "I don't overly enjoy it." Speaking honestly, I added, "I do not enjoy the crowds of people and loud music. But Leo can trust me to keep an eye out for anything ... funny, I guess. His daughter was helping him, but she married and moved away a few years ago. Right around the same time I dropped out of college a few towns away and stayed home to help my father recover from a heart attack while my mom worked. I decided family was more important than school at the time. So I worked on the weekends and at night when she was home. I always planned on returning to school, but time got away from me I guess. Looking back, it was the right decision. It could have been time lost that I'd never get back—with my parents, I mean. ..."

He barely let me catch my breath. "How about friends?" he asked.

"Don't have any, really." I shrugged. "All the other bartenders often hang out together. But I'm just there for the job, not to make friends. When the night is over I come home to silence happily. I have never been very social, even in school." I sighed and stopped fighting the urge to be so guarded. It was easy to talk to a stranger. "I never really fit in during my school years. High school was the worst. I think being an only child, or maybe always being at the shop with my mother and around other adults, made it hard for me to connect with kids my own age. I didn't like the girls in my school. All dramatic and waiting to hear and spread the latest gossip. I spent a lot of time studying instead of going to parties, which only made me more of an outsider. But it never bothered me. I enjoyed learning, discovering something new every day." I relaxed and placed my hands in my lap. I waited, and a small smile formed on his lips.

"And the boys?" he pressed.

My eyes fell to my lap and a knot formed in my stomach. "Boy," I corrected him. "Gavin." I shook my head. "Just Gavin ... we met sophomore year of high school when he moved here from Nebraska. I was asked to show him around the school his first day, and that was it. There was something different about him. He wasn't like all the other boys in school. Gavin didn't show off, acting all tough and superior. But he still made a lot of friends. He was one of the good guys, and we were together for three years. He was the only person who really knew me besides my parents. Probably would have spent the rest of my life with him." I tried not to think about that too much.

I coughed and then just blurted it out. "Senior year he went on spring break with some friends and was killed in a boating accident." Out of the corner of my eye, I could see Sorin straighten in the chair. "It was an all-male trip so I wasn't with him. All the guys went swimming in the ocean after dark, and a boat was out on the water when it shouldn't have been. Both parties were breaking beach rules by being there after dark. Gavin was resurfacing when the boat came near shore. Both were at fault. They said he was knocked out and drowned. It was too late by the time they found him and pulled him from the water. So that's it. ... The only three people I ever really loved are now gone. Each of them left me." I reached up and wiped my eyes before the tears could fall.

"I am sorry, Mia. I did not realize the extent of your loss." Sorin stood up, and I finally looked at him. "I should allow you to sleep now. It really has grown late." I could tell he regretted asking about me. The thought of being alone didn't bother me anymore now that I knew he would be upstairs, so I didn't argue with him. He slowly crossed to the door and then turned back at me. "Sleep well, Mia." He reached down, turned the lock on the doorknob, and shut off the light. Once in the hall, he pulled the door closed, and the lock clicked.

I just sat there in darkness and listened to the silence. I realized the rain had stopped, so I went to the window. I pulled back the heavy white lace curtain with pink roses and then the deep-pink curtain behind it. The clouds had cleared, and moonlight spilled into the room. I looked up at the sky; the moon was just shy of being full. Standing there looking into the backyard I could see the moonlight reached the trees at the bottom of the hill. The river that was on the other side of the trees drew quite a bit of wildlife to the area. On more than one occasion I had seen deer or a fox in the backyard near the tree line. I always looked for animals in the morning while getting ready for school. The past few years my sleeping habits had changed because of bartending on weekends. There had been fewer mornings with my parents.

My chest tightened, and I fought tears. I sat on the edge of the bed and slipped out of my jeans before crawling under the covers. I buried myself under the sheet and light quilt patterned in various shades of pink. The room was cooler than normal, and I realized Jennifer or Gina must have turned the air conditioning up because there were so many people in the house the today. I decided to wait till morning to adjust it.

I lay there and thought about life. How quickly a family could be shattered and never whole again. I didn't want to be without my parents. I wished I had been in the car with them. Maybe if I had gone with them they would still be here. Or maybe the accident still would have happened, but I would have died with them. The longer I lay there, the more I went over the possibilities in my head. It caused me to blame myself more and miss them more. I wanted to join them. It had become a vicious cycle I relived every day now.

Just before exhaustion took over I thought of Sorin upstairs. I knew it was foolish of me to invite someone I didn't know to stay in my house. I didn't care; a part of me was gradually valuing my life less and less. If I were lucky, he was a serial killer who would strike when the opportunity presented itself. What could be better than a weak, devastated single woman home alone? I wished he hadn't locked the guest room door, and I considered getting out of bed to leave it ajar. I knew how self-destructive I was becoming. I squeezed my eyes shut. The first words I'd heard Sorin speak ran through my mind. That first glimpse of his face; I had thought he was an angel. Stoic and beautiful and here to take me away. An angel of death. My dark angel, who left me unsatisfied. *Murderer,* I thought once more. Wishing him a cold-blooded killer, the hope of not waking up came over me. Finally, I drifted off, filled with mixed emotions. I slept through the few hours of darkness left and easily through most of the next day. The phone rang a few times, but I just shoved my head under a pillow.

Chapter 5

Some time passed, and my phone rang again. This time my head and body were too rested not to wake up in response. Each ring brought me out of my haze a little bit more. Finally, I tossed the pillow and blankets aside and went to the vanity across the room. I looked at the phone, focusing on the name flashing on the screen. I picked it up. "Yes, mama bear?" I said flatly.

There was a brief silence, and then Jennifer spoke. "I just wanted to check on you." Another pause. "I just want you to know you can call me if you need anything, Mia." She sounded sad.

I felt guilty for being rude. Softening my tone, I said, "Thank you, Jennifer. Thank you for checking on me. I will call if I need anything … I promise." I hoped I put her at ease, if only a little.

"I will give you a week to yourself, Mia," Jennifer continued. "Then we should get together. You should decide if you want to take over your mother's responsibilities. I'll show you a few of our new recipes for the bakery." She paused and sighed. "Just think about it for me … please."

The phone chimed; she had hung up. I set the phone back down and returned to the bed. I swiped my jeans off the floor and slid into them before heading to the kitchen. Walking lightly down the hall and listening for any sign of Sorin. Nothing. The kitchen was empty as I looked around. Everything looked exactly the same as the night before. I opened the fridge door and found the same. It was already late in the day, and I thought he would have been up for hours and surely eaten something by now. I let go of the refrigerator door. With a soft push it closed on its own.

I started to wonder if Sorin was even here. I saw his suitcase had been moved from the doorway. I walked to the opposite side of the kitchen but halted in the doorway. It took everything I had to go this far. I looked at the table, and relief washed over me. The pictures had been moved since yesterday. Jennifer had at least done that before leaving last night. I took a few more steps and could see all the way into the foyer and front room. I listened again: nothing. No television or muffled moving upstairs. I turned the thermostat setting and walked back to the kitchen. Sorin could still be sleeping. I had just woken up myself.

I looked at the clock on the wall. Most of the day had passed. Walking to the clock, I removed it. My father had hung it, so I was surprised by how heavy it was. I looked at it once more before carrying it away. It was as large as my torso and made out of cast iron with some copper accents. My father had brought it home as a gift for my mother years ago after she'd pointed it out at the local antique store. She had returned to buy it, but it had been sold. To my father, who hid it for at least two months until he gave it to her as a birthday present. I looked around trying to decide where to store it. I ended up sliding it in a gap between the refrigerator and the wall.

I looked down at it as I stepped back. Time had become a cruel thing. The clock only showed me the minutes and hours that passed without my parents. I didn't care what time it was—or what day even. I didn't need to be anywhere. I made my own schedule as far as my artwork was concerned.

Living in a small town, everyone knew about the accident. I was sure it had made the front page of the paper. For that reason, I hadn't collected the papers from the front porch in days. Everyone knew; I didn't expect any calls for me to paint a family portrait or fulfill any other requests for a while. Leo had hugged me yesterday, telling me not to worry about working the weekend shifts till I was ready. After all, he'd been my parents' friend before he was my boss.

I suddenly heard footsteps above and felt relieved to know Sorin was still here after all. I was about to figure out what to offer him to eat when I heard a door shut rather loudly, followed by the faint sound of water running. He must be taking a shower. I looked down at myself. I was wearing the same clothes as last night. A shower was a good idea. I went back to the guest room and stared at my pile of clothes. I pulled out the only other pair of jeans I had downstairs. Another pair of dark-washed jeans, some black boy shorts underwear. A pretty black lace bra and dark-plum ribbed tank top. It was still chilly inside but I planned to step outside and enjoy some warm air later.

I put all the clothes in a ball and took them to the bathroom. I dumped them on the bathroom counter, lifting my shirt over my head. I reached back to unhook my bra and stopped. The water overhead shut off, and a door slammed upstairs. I stepped farther from the bathroom door, shutting and locking it. I finished undressing and kicked my clothes to the corner. I brushed my teeth and let my hair down. The shower water slowly warmed up, and I adjusted the shower head to the rain setting. I let the water fall over me for awhile before washing my hair. Orange and other citrus scents filled the air in the bathroom. I washed and shaved with my favorite honey scented body wash. My mind began to drift as I finished shaving, and I nicked my knee. I didn't realize until the soap made the cut sting. Looking down at my leg, I watched the blood wash away.

I looked closely at the razor in my right hand and then at the inside of my left wrist. I inspected the blades but decided they couldn't possibly do enough damage. I tossed the razor over the top of the shower curtain. I heard it hit the sink and then bounce. I crumpled to the tub floor, pulling my knees to my chest and wrapping my arms around my legs. Waves of despair flooded over me, and I barely felt the water on my back. It was so unfair. I wanted to scream, to hit something, to destroy something. I felt destroyed and broken. I just sat there and cried.

Some time must have past; I started to shiver. The water had turned cool. I reached up and shut it off. Stepping out of the shower my teeth began to chatter as the cold air hit me. I dried off quickly and dressed, trying to warm up. I combed my hair, twisting it back pinning it into place. Looking in the mirror, I saw a few missed strands here and there. They hung in curling waves, one by my temple and a few at my neck. My eyes were a little puffy, and my cheeks had a few pink splotches from crying. I dabbed on some face cream and shut off the bathroom light as I left.

The guest room curtains were still open from the night before, and the sun had started to set. I looked at the sky: swirls of bright orange and pink made their way through the trees. It was a fiery sunset. I stood and watched the sky slowly change colors. Letting my mind go blank for once. I closed the curtains and rubbed the goose bumps on my arms. I went to the kitchen, sure that Sorin would be down by now. I was wrong, and just as before, nothing had been moved. I didn't hear any noise from the other rooms. I shivered again and went straight to the thermostat panel in the front room, adjusting the temperature further. I stood still as I passed the steps again; no sound as I walked through the dining room, into the kitchen, and past the guest room I was staying in.

I opened the patio doors and stepped outside. The air was cooler than expected, still heavy from the rain yesterday and last night. I left the screen open so some warmer air could fill the house. There were puddles of water on the outdoor furniture. I tilted one of the chairs, letting the water run off it. Watching the sky change, I eventually saw the colors fade. Everything turned dark. Sounds greeted me. Children playing a few houses away. A dog barked, and eventually the music of crickets started filling the air. The last rays of scant light disappeared behind the trees, and a mosquito buzzed near my ear. I waved it away and decided to go inside. I slid the door shut behind me, locking it.

As I walked in through one side of the kitchen, Sorin entered the other. He stopped and looked at me, and his brow wrinkled. I couldn't hear exactly what he said from across the room, but I made out some of the words. Something about my "color being worse" or maybe it was, "Could her color be worse?"

I took a few steps forward, feeling defensive folding my arms across my chest as he walked up to me. "I'm sorry. I didn't hear that clearly." I sounded obviously unimpressed.

"I said that is a flattering color on you. You look rested," he offered, but I knew he was lying.

My mouth filled with saliva again, and there was a bitter taste. I went to get a glass of water, taking two glasses out of the cupboard. I pressed them into the refrigerator door and let a few ice cubes fall in each. The stool moved, and Sorin sat down. I took two bottles of water from the counter and placed them between us. "How did you sleep?" I asked wondering, why he was so late waking up.

"The bed was wonderful," he stated.

I pushed the glass of ice cubes and one of the water bottles closer to him. I opened the other bottle and poured some water over the ice. "I can make you something to eat. You must be starving." I motioned to the fridge.

The corner of his mouth turned in that odd way I had noticed last time we talked. "I stepped out while you were sleeping, so I have already eaten. But thank you for the offer." His voice trailed off.

The bitter taste grew, and I drank half my glass of water. Lemon would help me get rid of the taste in my mouth. "Would you like some lemon for your water?" I asked, nodded toward his glass. Taking a lemon from the counter's fruit bowl, I put it on top of a cutting board I removed from a drawer.

"How did you sleep, Mia?" His voice was soft and caring. I took a knife from the wooden block in front of me and cut off the ends the ends of the lemon. I paused, thinking. *Sleep. Well, sleeping is easy. ... Waking up and living every day is another story.* "As well as expected, I suppose," I said flatly, cutting the lemon into thin slices. The citrus scent tickled my nose.

Sorin had more questions for me. "Why are you staying down here in the guest room?" He sounded curious. I halted the knife again. *Because I can't bring myself to go upstairs,* I thought, picturing my room, the wine-colored walls plastered with photos of my parents and me. Twenty-three years of memories stored in one room. Each picture ran through my head. My mother and I at a spa day, green seaweed masks and cucumber over our eyes. She had slipped her camera to one of the aestheticians. My parents and I at my high school graduation; I was between them, wearing my purple cap and gown. The three of us at a beach in Daytona two summers ago, the sun setting behind us. ...

I looked down at the knife in my hand. I let go of the lemon and turned my left hand palm up. My eyes studied my wrist, the bruises from the day before had faded some. I made a fist and saw a vein rise. I looked back at the knife, tracing the blade with my eyes. "Sorin, you are not a doctor, correct?" It came out just above a whisper.

"No." His voice growled, and I jumped a little. I blinked and finished cutting the last part of the lemon. He had saved my mother years ago. But she had wanted to live; I didn't. "Mia ... some lemon, please!" His voice boomed, and I dropped the knife and spun around. Sorin sat, rubbing his temples and glaring at me. I reached back and picked up a few lemon slices. I gently slid two into my glass, shooting him a foul look as I plopped the other two in his glass. They made a small splash.

"You don't have to yell," I retorted.

He relaxed and glanced back at the dining room doorway. "Come join me in the other room, and we will sit and talk." His voice could just flow through me at times. It was starting to irritate me. He stood up and came around the counter. I turned toward him on my stool, waiting to see what he was doing. I thought he was going to the refrigerator for some food after all. But he passed it and walked right up to me. He stopped just a foot away.

Sorin's gaze passed over me, and he raised a hand to my face. His fingers traced my jaw, stopping at my chin. I could smell that wonderful scent of sandalwood and something else so familiar. My head started feeling light. This was definitely irritating. I wasn't a young schoolgirl anymore. Even in school I was not affected so easily when a boy showed some attention. His fingers curled under my chin, and he lifted my face up to his. He whispered my name, and I blinked a few times, trying to clear my head. But his eyes were pale blue pools in front of me, and I was drowning in them. He said my name again, but it barely registered. My eyes grew heavy, and I struggled to keep them open.

I swear he fought a smile before he leaned in. A shiver climbed my spine. "Mia, go sit and relax in the other room. I will bring you some food. You will eat and tell me more about yourself." His voice purred like before. It made me melt; my brain had become obsolete. Just like last night when he talked to me. I seemed to absentmindedly obey, trying to say "yes or okay. Anything. But my lips wouldn't move. A pitiful cross between a moan and whimper was all that echoed in my head. I couldn't really tell if the sound had escaped my lips.

Sorin smiled against my face. I could feel his facial muscles change, and a light chuckle escaped him. "Go on … I will join you before you know it." He gently turned me and gave me a light push off the stool. I felt sedated, like I was floating, even a little drunk. I couldn't finish a thought, much less speak; I could hardly walk. I was moving, though—the walls were passing me. First the dining room, and then the foyer as I passed the stairs. I felt like maybe I was in a dream, all fuzzy and warm. I slapped at the light switch as I passed it. The light over the fireplace on the far wall lit up, and I moved on. I continued to the larger of the two couches and sat in the corner facing the kitchen. I swung my legs up and stretched them out in front of me. Grabbing a blanket off the back of the couch, I laid it across the lower half of my body. I smoothed the blanket, and a moment later the rest of the room illuminated fully.

Sorin's hand instantly appeared in front of me with a plate of food. My head bobbed to his face and then back to the plate. He put it on my lap, sat in the opposite corner, and rested his arm on the back of the sofa. His body was turned in my direction, with one leg bent and resting near my feet. The other leg hung over the side. Sorin lifted his left hand and pressed his fist against his temple. He just sat there, looking relaxed. "Eat, Mia," he said softly, picking up a cinnamon roll with his free hand. He held it in front of me until I took it from him.

I slowly ate it, tearing it apart. I glanced up at him between bites. Every time I looked up, his eyes were on me. But never the same place. I saw Sorin looking down at my feet peeking out from under the blanket. Another time it was my hands while I was tearing the roll apart. Then his eyes followed the food to my mouth, watching me lick my lips free of the icing. The way he watched me should have caused my heart to race. But I felt calm, like the world didn't exist at the moment. After the roll was gone, Sorin turned the plate so some grapes and strawberries were in front of me. I picked them up and ate them. After the third or fourth one, my head started to clear. The fog slowly lifted, and I took a few deep breaths. It helped; I no longer felt sedated. So I took a few more deep breaths and blew them out slowly. I looked at Sorin. This time his eyes were locked somewhere between my neck and collarbone. I started to gather my thoughts and looked down at my plate now half empty. Even though I hadn't wanted to eat anything. I felt how at ease my body was. The last of the cobwebs lifted from my head.

My true emotions slowly bubbled up inside me. It was déjà vu—exactly like last night. Sorin talked to me in a voice I could feel caress my skin. I even began to feel a part of me crave it. He spoke, and I agreed to whatever he requested. My eyes darted forward, narrowing and settling on him. He instantly lifted his gaze from my neck. I could feel my body begin to tense as I tried to figure out what was happening to me. Sorin's eyes widened a little, and he lifted his head from where it rested against his hand. I looked at the food and thought for a minute. No, it wasn't the food. I always became dizzy before I ate, not after. Tonight all I'd had was a glass of water, so it wasn't strange that I felt light-headed, given how many hours it had been since I'd last eaten. But something still didn't add up. The more I thought about it, the more my frustration increased.

I looked back at Sorin. His arm fell from the back of the sofa, and his back straightened. "What are you doing to me?" I accused.

He shifted slightly, and his eyes became piercing. The smooth skin between his eyes tensed and wrinkled. His lips pressed tight and he blurted out, "I have no idea to what you are referring, Mia."

My stomach lurched, and that horrible taste filled my mouth. Bitter, the flavor of something metallic or medicinal. I grabbed my stomach and shrieked. "The hell you don't! What is this awful taste? ... Did you do something to my food?" I was starting to panic. I felt out control.

A combination of concern and surprise washed over his face. Sorin moved toward me.

"No!" I yelled, jerking my knees up to my chest and holding both hands out to stop him. The plate fell from my lap and hit the floor, neither one of us even flinching at the sound.

He moved back to his side and stared at me. I wrapped both my arms around my midsection, laying my head on my knees.

He finally spoke. "Mia, I promise you ... I put nothing in your food. Nor in your drink." His voice was filled with anguish.

I didn't want to hear it, but it was unmistakable. It wasn't the thought of him poisoning me that upset me so much. Just last night, a part of me had wished he would murder me as I slept. But the absolute calm he made me feel was unnerving. It was beyond calm; I became numb. I couldn't do this—feel the worst pain and loss of my life one minute, only to be totally calm and oblivious the next. I felt myself start to slowly rock back and forth. All Sorin had to do was look into my eyes and whisper into my ear, causing me to feel peaceful. I felt the cushion shift near my feet and I screamed no into my knees as I continued to sway my body.

It wasn't fair that a stranger could affect me like this. Sorin could make me briefly not mind continuing to live without my parents. There were moments that he didn't feel like a stranger at all; it was as if I had always known him. A small part of me craved how he made me feel, and it made me ache for more. But he would eventually leave, just like everyone else. I would be abandoned yet again. He would leave and take that wonderful feeling of peace with him. I was so angry and frustrated that my eyes stung with tears. I fought them the best I could. He moved closer again, placing his hands on my shoulders, gently squeezing them. My body stilled, and a whimper escaped me. He moved closer, sliding an arm between me and the sofa. Sorin's other arm slipped under my knees. In a soft fluid movement he brought me to him. Laying my legs across his lap, he pressed my body against his. I couldn't help but mold to him. Protectively wrapped in his arms, my head rested at the top of his chest.

"*Shh,* Mia … just breathe. Take a few deep breaths, and it will be better. I promise." He said it slowly, softly, as he kissed my temple. I knew if I did as he said everything would melt away, and my mood would totally change. His sweater was soft against my face, a few tears absorbed into it. Sorin's scent filled my nose. *His scent,* I thought and pulled away from him. I pressed a palm to his chest. I shook my head and kept him at arm's length. Sorin's arm fell from around my body, and he rested it just above my knee.

My head was already spinning, and I started to babble, fighting the jumbled mess that filled my head. "No!" I yelled, shoving my hand harder against his chest. "'Cause it's your scent that does it." My eyes moved over his body, my hand dropping away. I shook my head and lowered my tone. "No, it's your voice … that makes me … it makes me fade." My voice cracked. I felt utterly confused. I looked at his mouth, studied his full pale lips. I closed my eyes and could hear words he had spoken to me earlier and last night. Suddenly I was imagining his eyes, deep ice-blue pools, hypnotizing me. My eyes shot open and collided with his. "Is that it?" I accused in a low tone. "Are you hypnotizing me somehow?"

Sorin just sat there, one hand holding my calf on his lap. The other hand left my back and lay above my knee. His eyes were wild with emotions. He looked hurt, confused. His jaw flexed, and his lips pressed tighter, but he didn't say a word.

My face felt flushed and my hands became fists in my lap. "Talk!" I finally yelled at him. "Say something! Explain it … don't deny you are doing something to me."

Sorin's shoulders slumped a little, and his eyes fell to my knees. "I am sorry, Mia … truly." His voice was apologetic, sincere. His eyes left my knees and slowly lifted higher.

I turned my head away. I couldn't trust myself to look at him. I took a deep breath and tried to pull my emotions in. "Is it drugs?" I demanded.

"No," he assured me.

I relaxed a little. "Are you hypnotizing me somehow?" I turned my head back toward him but looked down at his hands. His right hand started to slowly massage my calf through the blanket.

"No." Sorin paused, and his hand stopped for a brief moment. "I am only trying to ease your pain. If only a little … for a short time." He chose his words carefully, drawing each one out. "It is forgivable, Mia. To let go of the pain in your heart for a moment or two." And then his voice changed to that soft, seductive tone that I had yet to ignore. "It is natural, Mia … to let go when it becomes too much." His hand crept up my thigh and covered my hands. I wanted to fight it, but my body betrayed me. My hands fell open and I slumped to my right.

I lay against the back of the couch, my face resting against the top. I closed my eyes. I could feel the frame pressing into my temple. It was uncomfortable, but my head felt too dizzy to move. Sorin slipped his hand between my face and the wooden frame. A cool palm cradled my face. His other hand left my calf and was gently moving the blanket from my lap onto the arm of the couch behind me. He rolled my head onto it with ease. Sorin's hands slid down my neck and out to my shoulders. Gingerly down my arms to my hands, which he placed in my lap. I felt limp—that same helpless, numb feeling. I screamed at myself in my head. *Fight it!* my inner voice kept repeating over and over. My head bobbed from side to side, and I fought to open my eyes.

"Sorin …" I breathed. His left hand rested on the spot just above my knee where it had been before. The right began kneading my calf through my jeans. "Sorin … stop …

please," I begged, fluttering my eyes open to look at him. "You're wrong." I said. "This isn't natural. I don't know you, and you don't know me. Yet I invited you to stay here. I have moments where I feel I've known you my whole life. A part of me craves whatever it is that you do to me. This isn't me: self-destructive and unable to control my own emotions. I'm not like that at all!" As I raised my voice, I looked into Sorin's eyes. "This is not … natural," I finished. Each word was a little louder, a little more pronounced, than the one before.

Slowly his cheeks lifted, and the corners of his mouth turned up into a smile. Not a big smile with all his teeth showing. But a smile with his lips closed, with his cheeks high and a tiny purse to his lips. Then his eyebrows lifted. Sorin's eyes brightened, and his face was even more beautiful than it had been when I'd first glimpsed him. He leaned toward me, and my heart skipped a beat. "Mia," he purred, as my head clouded further. "*This* is simply you and me." His eyes danced over my body and returned to meet mine. "*This* is what you truly want—calm and peace. And you allow me to do this for you. It is natural, the most natural desire on earth." He sat back and paused. "If you did not want this, if you did not long for a brief moment free of heartache … for me … it would not be." His shoulders eased and he propped his head on his fist in the same way he had earlier. He looked the most comfortable I had seen him. Like he belonged right here, had nowhere else to be but beside me.

My head swam. "Make it stop. Please make my head stop spinning." I pleaded in a weak voice that was all I could produce just then.

His smile faded, eyebrows smoothed. "Do you want it to pass? The haze, the warm calm you are currently experiencing?" He looked a little sad as he asked. He knew exactly what I was feeling. It was eerie. My body felt great; every muscle at ease. It was my head that was screaming, fighting. "Yes!" I pleaded and rolled my eyes closed. Sorin lifted my legs and moved farther away, all the way to the opposite side of the couch. The heels of my feet just reached his lap and stayed propped there. His hands gently closed around my naked feet. "Sorin?" I whispered, waiting for my head to magically clear.

"Just relax and take a few deep breaths. … It will pass if you want it to." His voice was empty, like a stranger giving me directions to a location. But I listened anyway. I kept my eyes closed. Head laid back and arms limp. I took a few deep breaths and paused. *A little better,* I thought to myself. Slowly his thumbs circled the bottom of my feet. I didn't mean to let it, but a moan escaped me. It felt great. I didn't normally wear high heels like I had the previous day. My feet were still tender from standing and walking so much in them. I took a few more deep breaths, and more fog lifted from my head. Sorin's thumbs continued: small circles over the pads under my toes. Then a smooth circle to my heel and back up. Every few minutes he would squeeze my whole foot and ease his hand to my ankle and back. Sorin continued his silence. I took a few more deep breaths and gently blew them past my lips. Finally my head cleared. Not completely, but enough for me to open my eyes. I lifted my head and looked over at him. Leaving my feet, his eyes met mine. We sat there, just staring at each other. Neither one of us knowing what to do or say. Both of us waited for the other to speak, to say anything. I had so many questions still screaming in the back of my mind. I struggled to choose the most dominant ones. Who was he really? Where was he from? What else had happened between him and my mother? My heart sank a little as I wondered how much longer he would stay here with me. I sighed, wanting to ask him all this, even if I was afraid of the answers that might follow.

Sorin's hands stopped and a thoughtful look crossed his face. "What is your favorite food, Mia?" He tried to sound light, relaxed. It took a second for the question to sink in, for me to grasp such a simple inquiry. "Please, Mia … your favorite food, favorite color, season, holiday … everything. I really do want to know everything about you." He was genuinely curious about me. Sorin looked at me, waiting, eager for me to answer.

I thought for a minute, trying to decide if I wanted to go along with mundane facts of my life. Or press about concerns I had and questions I wanted answered. It suddenly occurred to me that my head was clear. He wanted something from me and hadn't used that voice that flowed over and through me. I sat straight up, pressing my back against the arm of the sofa. He moved a little closer, letting my lower legs rest on his lap. "My favorite food, huh?" I repeated, still deciding which way I really wanted the conversation to go.

Sorin propped his left arm on the back of the couch again, resting his head on his fist. His other hand rested on my ankle, just under my jeans, gently touching my skin.

I rolled my eyes and made a disgusted sound as I agreed to talk about myself more. "Pizza," I stated. One of his eyebrows rose and his hand squeezed my leg. He wanted more than a one-word answer. "My favorite food is pizza because you can have it so many different ways. You can put meat on it, fruit, white sauce, tomato sauce, and multiple cheeses. You could go your whole life and probably not eat the same kind of pizza twice." I raised my chin. "Detailed enough for you?" I quipped.

Sorin actually shook his head, and my jaw went slack. "Almost … you failed to clarify which you enjoy most."

I sighed. "I like tomato and basil with provolone cheese." He nodded an approval. "You?" I shot back.

"I do not eat pizza," he replied. "What is your favorite color?" He offered a new question.

"Green … the darker the better. I like to wear it because my eyes are a mixture of colors. When I wear green they seem to follow." He smiled softly and seemed to enjoy the answer.

The questions continued, and so did the answers. Sorin just sat there contentedly, hanging on my every word. It had been so long since I'd sat and talked to anyone other than my parents—even longer with someone of the opposite sex closer to my own age. It felt comfortable, though.

If I would allow myself to, I could pour my heart out to him.

Chapter 6

"I don't do this," I finally blurted out as Sorin took a moment to think of another question. "I mean, I am not a sharing person. I don't chitchat or go out for coffee with the girls." Actually I hadn't had a deep meaningful conversation since Gavin, and that had been years ago. I started to think about Gavin and the few years I spent with him. We'd had so many conversations about hopes and dreams—mine and his. His had been cruelly cut short. Only a few of mine had been fulfilled. My body began to tense as I drifted deeper into memories of Gavin.

"Animal." Sorin suddenly threw the word out, snapping me back to the present. "Animal ... what is my favorite animal?" I questioned, sounding bored. He just nodded.

I looked off to the side and thought about it. "Skunks," I said sheepishly, waiting for him to make a repulsed face. But he didn't, so I explained. "Skunks, because they are so misunderstood. They only stink to protect themselves." I turned to my side and rolled up the blanket behind me, using it as a pillow. I lay my head down.

Sorin's forehead wrinkled. "Are you sleepy, Mia? Should I walk you to your room?" He asked, and lifted his head a little.

"No, not sleepy ... just relaxed. *Naturally* relaxed," I added for emphasis, not sure if he would catch my intentional accusation.

"Which season?" Sorin asked, ignoring my last comment.

"Spring—the rain, the growth ... everything is all fresh and new."

"Bird?" He softly smiled, and I rolled my eyes. Every time I thought it couldn't get more pointless, he asked about something simple. It seemed foolish to me, but then I realized he was just trying to pick easy topics. Unimportant things. He was trying to keep me relaxed and in the moment.

"Peacock" I finally said. "They are bright and colorful. The males are the ones with the vivid colors, and they show their feathers only during mating season."

There was a brief silence as he searched for something he hadn't already asked. "Flower?" he asked, and my heart dropped. Water lilies filled my mind's eye, and I remembered yesterday's dream. The dock surrounded by lily pads. My dad. Saving me. Always there for me. ... My heart ached, and tears began to fill my vision.

"Food," I heard him say quickly, and I blinked.

"You already asked about my favorite food, Sorin," I whispered in a hollow voice.

He stood up and offered me his hand. "Food," he said again. "You should ... we should eat." He sounded determined. I was under the impression he wasn't going to accept a no from me. I put my hand in his and swung my feet around as he helped me up.

As I stepped toward him a grape squished between my toes. "Yuck!" I complained as I looked down. I was about to kneel down to clean up the discarded plate and fruit at my feet—the one we'd left untended—but Sorin caught my elbow. "I will tend to this, Mia. Go get something to eat." He guided me past him as he spoke. I was aggravated. Between recalling more of my dream, the grape pieces between my toes, and his ordering to eat, I couldn't mask my irritation. "Good idea!" I retorted angrily. "From now on I will handle my own food."

I didn't look back at him as I walked to the kitchen. I yanked open the fridge door, pulled out a container of strawberries, and plated them. I searched the refrigerator door, grabbing the carrot juice. I poured myself a glass and drank it. Sorin returned with the plate covered with pieces of smashed fruit. I moved so he could put the plate in the sink. As he passed the refrigerator he paused and turned back to me.

"Why did you remove the clock?" His head tilted in that odd way I was beginning to notice more.

I put my empty glass in the sink and sat on the stool, setting the plate of strawberries in front of me. I turned my head to the side and saw the edge of the clock near his feet. "I have no use for it right now ... I don't need to know what time it is. I don't have anywhere to be." I looked up at his face, inhaling deeply. "How about you ... do you have somewhere to be?" *There,* I thought, *I finally asked.* I held my breath and waited for him to answer, watching as he circled the island and took the seat across from me.

Sorin's hands crossed the cool dark marble to touch mine. He took my hands in his, caressing them. "Mia ... I have nowhere to be but here with you." He meant it. I exhaled, relieved, but a part of me still doubted.

"But for how long?" I pressed.

As soon as the words left my mouth Sorin answered. "As long as you want." With that, he raised my hands to his

67

lips as he leaned forward and kissed my fingers. My heart jumped, and my cheeks warmed. I pulled my hands back, moving them down to my lap. I hadn't blushed in a really long time. It was embarrassing to think about how long it had been since anyone had touched me like that.

I hadn't been with a guy since Gavin in our senior year of high school. Thinking of him didn't hurt quite as much as it used to. It had been five years now. Five years since a man held my hands and made me blush. After Gavin died I just never felt interested in being in a relationship or even in dating. With every month that went by it just became less of a priority. It hadn't helped that every weekend for the past three years at least one drunk guy had offered to take me back to his place at closing time.

The glass plate squeaked over the counter, and I looked down. Sorin held out a strawberry, and without a thought I took it from him. "What do you do for a living?" I took advantage of a moment where he no longer asked me question after question. I looked up when he didn't answer. His back was stiff, and he looked like he had to think about it. "It is not a trick question, Sorin," I half teased.

His eyes focused on me, and I thought maybe he hadn't been listening. "Sorry. I sell antiques for a living." He didn't sound like his usual confident self, but then he relaxed a little. "I travel and make my own work schedule." His eyes brightened "I have nowhere to be but here with you, I promise." He smiled lightly.

I shrugged. It wasn't what I had meant by the question. But his answer was reassuring. He reached down to pick up another strawberry for me, quickly wishing he hadn't.

I slapped his hand away and shoved the plate to his side of the counter. He backed away from it and looked at me, confused.

"What? … You eat something," I said rather loudly, picking up a strawberry for him to eat. "You want to tell me to eat. Practically shove food in my face. But it's not acceptable the other way around? What a hypocrite." I dropped the fruit on the plate and crossed my arms. Waiting and watching, all he did was stare at the plate.

Finally Sorin looked up at me and shook his head. "No," he replied.

"No?!" I said even louder. "Why not?"

His frame eased from its tension, and his lips turned up a little. "I cannot … I am allergic. I would become very ill." His smile increased a little more. "Do you want me to fall ill, Mia?" Sorin's voice was taunting me, catching me by surprise.

I leaned forward onto the marble, and my shoulders fell. I felt awful and apologized quickly. "I'm sorry. I didn't know … I mean, I have never actually met anyone allergic to strawberries." I rambled. "I was just tired of you forcing food on me."

He picked up the plate and walked around to put it in the sink. I heard it clink against the other plate. "There is no need to dwell on it, Mia." He sounded a little amused. "I will stop trying to make you eat. I mean well. It was my attempt at keeping you from wasting away." Sorin's hands squeezed my upper arms, and he kissed the back of my head. Walking past me to the doorway, he looked back at me. "Come, I will walk you to your room." He stuck his elbow out for me to take. We had spent hours talking in the front room; it was now the early hours of the morning.

I sighed and slid off the stool to join him. I tucked my hand into the crease of his elbow, and we walked together. At the doorway to the guest room I released his arm and entered. The light flicked on, and I turned back to him. Sorin just lingered in the doorway. I couldn't help but remind him. "You have been in this room before." I looked to the window. It was still dark outside. "It is pretty early still; the sun isn't even up yet. Keep my company till I fall to sleep. I have a million questions for you to answer … please," I cajoled.

His head tilted slightly, and he studied me for a moment. Finally he gave me a soft smile and joined me. I went to the bathroom and washed my face. I moistened a wash cloth and cleaned my foot where it still felt sticky from stepping on the grape. I pulled the few pins out of my hair and shook it till the waves of hair spilled over my shoulders. I came out into the room and turned the lamp on. As I shut off the overhead light, I realized the room was still pretty well lit. Sorin was sitting in the chair from last night, his legs resting on the bed. I walked to the opposite side of the bed and paused. I was running out of clean clothes again.

I felt nervous as I reached down to undo my jeans. As soon as my fingers touched the metal button, Sorin's head lifted. He kept his eyes on the ceiling. I shouldn't have been surprised. He had behaved mostly gentlemanly these past two days. I was glad; it just wasn't common anymore. Any other male would have eagerly watched me undress. I attributed it to his being foreign. I stepped out of my jeans and crawled into bed under the covers. I lay on my side, facing him and coughing lightly.

He looked at me and grinned. "Mia, share an amusing story from your past." Sorin sounded relaxed.

"More about me?" I moaned and fluffed my pillow before laying my head back on it. I thought for a moment. "When I was six or seven, my parents took me camping for the first time. The last morning of the trip I heard something rustling outside the tent. My parents were already up and out fixing breakfast. So I unzipped the tent and stepped out." I paused, picturing everything in my head. "There were two baby skunks behind our tent near some trees." A light chuckle left me as I remembered what followed. "They were the cutest little black and white tufts of fur. Unfortunately, I had it in my head that I wanted to take one home as a pet. I was convinced they wouldn't spray me because I was friendly. So I started chasing them. My parents must have heard me calling them, because suddenly my mother was shrieking. My father scooped me up before I could scare them and cause them to defend themselves." I rolled my eyes. "They didn't take me camping the following summer. But I have had a soft spot for skunks ever since."

Sorin smiled a crooked grin. "You were a fearless little one." He chuckled. Even though I had slept most of the previous day I was starting to feel drowsy. I sat up to shut off the lamp on the nightstand, intending to just talk in the dark. Sorin caught my wrist before I could twist the knob. My eyes darted from their destination to his face, and he let go of my hand. I lay back down, not sure what to say.

"I will shut it off when you fall asleep," he assured me. I rolled onto my back and looked at the ceiling. I surmised he wanted to watch me drift off to sleep. I thought about it—him sitting there watching over me. He had done it before. It did make my stomach flutter a little, and I found comfort in it. Sorin broke the silence. "Mia?" His tone was low, unsure. He was probably curious if I was paying attention. "*Hmm?*" was all I managed. My eyes were getting heavy. He continued, his voice cautious. "Mia ... this is not your bedroom." It was a question, but it came out as a statement. "Why do you sleep here, in this room?"

I closed my eyes and tried not to tense up. I had told him I was staying in the downstairs guest room. Plus, I hadn't considered that Sorin might wander into my real bedroom last night while searching for the upstairs guest room.

"No," I said after a minute or two. This is not my room. Mine is upstairs. This one has all my old furniture and bedding, though." I paused, trying to find the strength to continue. To enter into a deep and personal conversation. "The truth is, I'm just not ready to go upstairs yet ... to see the pictures on the hallway walls. See my parents' bedroom door at the top of the steps. I have told myself for days now, 'maybe tomorrow.' And then tomorrow comes and goes. I had to ask Kayla to go upstairs and get me a dress and shoes for the service. ... Maybe tomorrow." My stomach tightened at the thought, and my eyes felt moist as tears began to build. I didn't want to think about it anymore; I just wanted to fall asleep and be oblivious.

The bed shifted a little, but I was too close to sleep to open my eyes. Sorin kissed my forehead and whispered

near my temple. "Sleep now, Mia … let go and fade away."
His voice made me imagine warm snowflakes. Big beautiful
fluffy snowflakes—that somehow felt magically warm—
falling all around me. Sorin's words fell on my skin and melted
over me, warm and relaxing. I was torn—a part of me knew
this was not real. This feeling flowing over my body when he
spoke like this. But a part of me now longed for it. To drift
away, to slip into the quiet darkness and leave reality. Sleep
had become a form of death to me this past week. One I
didn't want to wake up from. I did let go, allowing myself to
fade away into the quiet darkness.

Chapter 7

I heard children screaming, excited and happy. I stirred and opened my eyes, turning toward the curtains. It was soon after dawn, just a little light coming through the window. I rolled out of bed and pulled on my jeans from the night before. I grabbed all my clothes from the floor and carried them to the laundry room. Once the wash cycle began I continued to the patio door. I stepped out and closed it behind me. The air was fresh and cool. I rested my elbows on the wooden railing and looked a few yards over. A small group of children were running around. Giggling and grabbing at the air. I looked closer and saw them, tiny quick flashes. I stood and glanced down at the tree line, where fireflies flickered. The sun had not just risen, it was about to set. Had I really slept the day away—again? It explained why I didn't feel fatigued after just a few hours of sleep. I leaned forward onto the railing and watched the children for a long time. I envied their innocence, the joy they filled the air with.

My stomach growled, and I went back inside. I stopped at the washer, hearing the spin cycle. I would return to it later. I expected to find Sorin in the kitchen or at least hear the television going. But just like the night before, there was no noise and no footsteps. Just silence all around the house. Just because I'd slept the day away didn't mean Sorin had. Why hadn't he woken me up? I started to worry that maybe he had turned in for the night. I pulled a plate of food from the fridge and picked at it as I stood at the counter. I ate only what I thought would quiet my stomach, still not really having an appetite. I threw the rest away and rinsed the plate. Water splashed onto my shirt. I looked down at my clothes and decided it was time to get something new to wear.

I stood up, convincing myself I could go upstairs. Just a quick trip to my room; grab some clothes and return to the downstairs. My legs felt heavy but moved anyway. I crossed the dining room into the foyer and paused, careful not to look up. I put my hand on the railing and slowly climbed the steps, looking down the whole time. Finally the last step was under me, and I turned right, toward my room. I kept my eyes down until I got to my door and stepped inside. I turned the light on and went straight to my dresser. I pulled out a few more lightweight shirts and a few pairs of socks. I grabbed my last two pairs of jeans, and then went to my closet. I threw a pair of sandals onto the pile I held. Going back to my dresser, I opened the bottom drawer and pulled out a pair of pajama bottoms. My hand brushed up against something soft and silky. I lowered myself to the floor and tucked my legs under me. I let my pile of clothes fall to the floor beside me. I brushed the other cotton pajamas to the side of the drawer.

There lay the little black nightgown I had made a special trip to the mall for years ago. I looped my fingers through the thin straps and lifted it up to admire. The pretty pink tag still hung daintily off to the side. I had bought it the first day Gavin was off on his trip with the guys. It had sat here buried under my pajamas for years now. It was made of soft black silk. It had fallen just above my knees when I tried it on and looked at my reflection in the dressing room mirror.

The front went down to a low V and the back did the same, stopping just below the small of my back.

Again I thought about how long it had been since I'd been with a man. Felt his hands on my body, his mouth on mine. My hands dropped to the layer of silk draped over my lap. For the first time in a long while I allowed myself to remember what it was like. Making love to Gavin, sharing everything you are. So intimate and exposed. I closed my eyes and thought of Sorin, the past few days with him. I recalled the first time I opened my eyes and saw his face. I thought he was an angel. His wonderful smell, his voice, his ice-blue eyes. My stomach fluttered a little. I looked back down at the nightgown. *No more "tomorrow"!* I thought. Why wait for the next day to act? Life had clearly shown me that tomorrow may not come.

Sorin had been a gentleman the past few days. Never made me feel uncomfortable. When he touched me, it was always in a gentle, caring way. He even looked away when I slipped out of my jeans before crawling to bed. Nothing had been inappropriate between us. My heart had skipped a beat once or twice. I relived his hand caressing my feet, massaging my calf. I sighed and let myself continue to imagine his hands touching me. Caressing other parts of my body. Butterflies slowly filled my stomach. What if there wasn't a tomorrow? What would I do tonight—right now? It wasn't unheard of, a woman turning to a man for comfort. To lose herself for a night or two, even with a stranger. I imagined he would be just as gentle and attentive in the bedroom. ...

There was a thud, and I jumped, my head shooting past my open door to the hallway. I threw the nightgown onto the pile of clothes and stood up. I shoved the bottom drawer shut with my foot and turned around. I turned off my light and shut my door behind me. I looked back down at the cream carpet on the hallway floor. I walked past my parents' room and the stairs to the attic. I stepped quietly and stood outside the guest room door. No light came out from underneath the frame. I didn't hear movement, so I leaned closer. Suddenly the shower turned on. Had Sorin been gone all day, or was he just getting up? I turned, put my eyes to the floor, and returned downstairs.

I rushed to the guest room that had become my refuge and dumped the pile of clothes onto the foot of the bed. I went to take a shower, leaving the bathroom light off but the door open. The light from the room drifted in. I undressed, tossing my clothes to the corner of the bathroom. I washed my hair, enjoying the orange scent. Lathered the honey-scented body wash over myself and shaved, careful not to cut myself this time. After I dried off and wrapped a towel around my body I walked to the foot of the bed. I stood there and stared at the pile of clothes. The nightgown had slipped to the floor. I picked it up and carried it to the bathroom. I placed the shimmer of silk on the counter in front of the mirror and gently trimmed the tag away. I stepped back and looked in the mirror. A distorted blur reflected back. I turned the light on and used the towel wrapped around me to wipe the condensation from the mirror.

I studied my reflection, hardly recognizing it. My stomach twisted, and I felt sick. My eyes looked flat, vacant. Had Sorin really commented on my color last night? My skin was pale. The tan I had acquired two weeks ago while painting a tree outdoors had faded. Running a hand over my abdomen, it felt strange, empty. ... I felt empty. My cheeks looked hollow, and I frowned. I remembered what Sorin had said. "I was only trying to keep you from wasting away." Was that how he saw me? Skin and bones. Pale and empty. That's what was staring back at me—a shell of my former self.

I crumpled to the floor and clutched the towel to my chest. I lifted the damp plush cotton to my face and screamed into it. My head stared to spin. Who had I become? This wasn't me. A week ago I was strong, independent, in control, content, happy ... loved. Where was that woman, I wondered. Would I find her again, or was she lost forever? I hated the tears that stung my eyes. The very act of crying was something I now loathed. It was all I seemed to do. I was never emotional like other girls. Never cried to get what I wanted with my parents. Never did it to get out of a speeding ticket. I rarely cried before the accident. Now it had become a daily occurrence, and I hated it. I wanted it to be over, this pain inside. The constant ache in my heart and soul. I wanted to feel something else—anything else.

Frustrated, I kicked the bathroom cupboard door in front of me, letting out another scream. The nightgown fell off the countertop above me and landed at my feet. I reached out for it, running my fingers over the soft smooth silk. I wanted to feel something other than anguish. I thought of Sorin's voice. The one he used that could make me drift off.

Wonderfully fade away to a complete peace. I thought of his lips, his hands on me. …

My thoughts rapidly spun out of control. I fantasized about how his hands would feel exploring my body. I envisioned his fingers tracing my face, down my neck, lightly over my collarbone. If Sorin could affect me so easily at times with his eyes and voice, I wanted to know what he could do to me with his body. I imagined him leaving a path of soft kisses over my skin. He could heal this hurt inside me, help me forget. …

In that instant, I decided. I stood up and slid the nightgown on. The straps crossed against my back. All the pain inside me, all the sorrow, suddenly turned into determination. I wanted to feel his arms around me. I wanted to feel a million butterflies inside. I longed for my heart to race and feel excited about something again.

Leaving the guest room I headed upstairs, images of us in each other's arms filling my head the whole way there. The closer I got to his door, the more graphic my thoughts became. My cheeks flushed, and my heart began to beat faster. Suddenly I was outside his door, about to burst in and throw myself at him. My hand on the doorknob. What if he rejected me? It was a real possibility, right? No, what man would turn away a young, willing, barely dressed woman? I exhaled a deep breath. That outcome was absurd. But I did decide to change my approach.

Still no light from under the doorway. I turned the knob slowly and opened the door just enough for me to slip through. The curtains were darker in this guest room, and less moonlight came through them. It was difficult to make out the shape of the bed in the dark. I stepped lightly toward it, until my knee bumped the wooden frame under the comforter. I leaned over, searching for the edge of the bedding and then slowly pulling it back. I slipped under the sheet and lay on my side, facing him.

I took a deep breath and tried to calm myself. I was now nervous, my body lightly shaking as I reached out under the blanket. I was planning on caressing his chest or back. I kept waiting for my hand to come into contact with his skin. I reached farther. Nothing. I slowly adjusted my body closer to his side of the bed. I took another deep breath and reached farther. Then I felt it. The edge of the bed. My heart sank.

I threw back the covers and rushed to the light switch, flipping it on. The room was empty and in perfect condition. Sorin's clothes weren't lying around. No books were removed from the shelf near the bed. No cell phone, no keys, no bag with his belongings. He was gone—just the left without even saying good-bye.

"He promised," I said out loud. "He said he would stay as long as I wanted." The same thought kept repeating in my head: *He left. I've been abandoned again.*

I shut off the upstairs guest room light and slowly descended the stairs to my current room. I felt hopeless. Having Sorin near me these few past days had brought me some comfort. I had found peace for a few minutes, even if how that sense of peace came about was suspicious. I reached my current room, turned the light on, and sat on the foot of the bed.

The past week crashed in on me. My parents here one day and then abruptly gone, ripped from my life. Sorin entering my life, compassionate and caring … or so I thought. He chose to leave me, to just pack and go. I was alone, no one to help me drift off to sleep. Comfort me in some mysterious way. My eyes wandered around the room. I felt rejected and alone. I didn't want to be aware of all this current pain; I didn't want to be aware, period. Having just woken up a little over an hour ago, trying to go back to sleep now naturally would be impossible. I considered going to the kitchen and drowning myself in a bottle of wine. But I'd never really liked the taste of alcohol. Probably why Leo trusted me working in his establishment as a bartender. He knew I never helped myself to drinks on the side.

My eyes drifted, resting on a prescription bottle sitting on the vanity across the room. I had forgotten all about it. Gina had left it for me the first night after we'd come back from the hospital. It was half her prescription for sleeping pills. She had said she had more at home, and if I really needed to take one, I should; it would help me sleep. Gina had also warned me they were pretty strong and not to drive after taking one. I crossed the room and picked up the bottle. Other than an occasional aspirin for a headache, I avoided any kind of medicine. I had viewed these pills as a false security or comfort, a loss of control which now was ironic. I hadn't given the pills a second thought. Until now. But whatever it was that Sorin did to me was exactly what I had avoided up to now. I read the label: Gina's name and address. Bright yellow stickers lined the side of the bottle. A circle with a plate of food and an X over a car.

Gina really was distraught the first night; we all had trouble going to sleep. I pictured her comforting Jenny. For twins, they couldn't have looked more unalike; they were fraternal twins, not identical, but they didn't even look like sisters. Gina had brown hair and brown eyes. Her skin appeared to hold a summer tan even in the middle of winter. The total opposite of blonde, blue-eyed Jennifer. But Gina was just as sweet and caring as her twin sister. She took care of the business part of the coffee shop. She did the schedules, payroll, and product orders. I wasn't surprised that she needed a sleep aid once in awhile.

The dosage said one pill, and Gina had given me the impression that would be plenty. I put a single pill in my palm and set the bottle back down on the vanity. A glass of water still sat on my nightstand, and I swallowed the water to wash down the pill. I crawled under the sheet, lay still in the bed, and waited for the darkness to embrace me. I reflected on my life while I waited. I was all alone, with nobody to comfort me. No one to share myself with tomorrow. *Tomorrow,* I thought. *Why continue into yet another day? Only to feel abandoned, rejected?* Another day wandering around a now-empty house.

I didn't have to suffer through another day, wondering how many more days would pass till the pain eased. I really didn't want to keep going; I felt devoid of any worth. I stared at the bottle of pills again and decided I wanted to go to sleep and not wake up. I flung the sheet back and started across the room. My head spun, and I knew the single pill was entering my system as I felt the first of its effects. I rushed myself across the room and slammed into the vanity. A few bottles toppled over, and the phone bumped into the bottle of pills. I picked up the phone and tossed it across the room. I wouldn't be changing my mind.

Twisting the lid off the bottle, I dumped the full contents into my hand. I briefly felt guilty for the false strength I must have conveyed—enough for Gina to trust me with her prescription. She would blame herself. But I couldn't think about that. I lifted the pills to my mouth, intending to ingest every last one and be done with this misery that had become my life.

Chapter 8

I heard the door crash open. Suddenly the pills were flying into the air, and Sorin was yelling at me, shaking me. He had knocked the pills out of my hand and grabbed me by the shoulders. "What are you doing, Mia?" He growled, inches from my face.

I was speechless, thinking he had left without as much as a good-bye. For him to be right in front of me, yelling at me, was jarring. "I thought … you left," was all I could manage to whisper.

Sorin's eyes were piercing, his face full of rage. My heart felt like it was about to pound out of my chest. I had the fleeting thought he might injure me himself. "How many?" he yelled, shaking me. My head tingled. I didn't understand what he was asking. "How many pills did you take, Mia?" Holding me at arm's length, Sorin's eyes searched the confetti of pills at our feet. He looked back up and quickly surveyed me.

I tried to gather my thoughts. Pulling away slightly, I attempted to free myself from his grasp. But Sorin pulled me against his body with such force that it knocked the air right out of me. He gritted his teeth and buried his face in my neck, inhaling deeply a few times. Was he really smelling me? I started shoving him away again, but the pill I had swallowed was starting to cause the room to spin. "Let go of me!" I finally shouted at him.

A growl escaped him, and he yelled again, "How many pills did you take?" When I didn't answer, Sorin's eyes shot past me to the bathroom behind me. Before I could wiggle loose, he caught me by the wrist and dragged me into the bathroom. He flipped the light switch on and put the toilet seat up. I jerked against his grasp, screaming, "No!" Sorin wanted me to make myself sick, to vomit over one little pill. "Do it," he demanded through clenched teeth, starting to pull me closer.

"One!" I yelled. "I swear ... I only took one." I was frantic to get away from him. Again, he pulled me against him and buried his face and my neck. He swore something against my skin, his grip crushing my wrist. "You're hurting me!" I cried out. He slammed the toilet lid back down and forced me to sit. In one swift motion Sorin moved to the bathroom door, closed it, and sat down in front of it, facing me. He was blocking me from leaving, and for the first time I felt scared.

I looked down at myself and realized I was still wearing the black silk nightgown. My cheeks started to warm. Uncoordinated, I slid to the bathroom floor, wedging myself between the toilet and bathroom cupboard. I awkwardly flung my hand over my head and grabbed for a towel above me. I finally felt one and pulled it down to cover myself with. I didn't take my eyes off of Sorin, his head leaning back against the bathroom door. His left leg was bent up with his left arm resting on it. His eyes were shut and frown lines filled his forehead. Go away!" I managed, shaking and feeling desperate.

Sorin lifted his head and opened his eyes. "Mia, if I could leave you ... I swear I would." His tone was heavy and bitter. "This ... you are almost too much for even me to handle." He rubbed his temple and closed his eyes briefly. His shoulders relaxed slowly, and he lowered his hand from his temple. Sorin's face softened slightly, and he shook his head.

"Maybe I went about this all wrong … I mean, maybe I should have just told you the truth." I couldn't make sense of his words. "I just thought it would be too much for you … so soon after the loss of your parents." He rested his head back against the door again. Looking pensive, he paused for a minute. His eyes traveled over me, and I brought my knees up to my body, increasingly thankful that the oversized towel covered me.

Finally he spoke. "Mia … I need to tell you something. I want you to truly listen to the words I am about to say … and believe me." My head was starting to tingle more, and my body was slowly relaxing against my will. I struggled to focus. "Mia, I am not like you. … I mean I am very different from your kind." Sorin spoke softly, cautious. "It is difficult for me to explain exactly what I am to you." He glanced at the floor, searching again for the right thing to say. His words started to sink into my head, and I tried to decipher their meaning: "not like you"; "different from your kind." What was he trying to explain? My head started to get really foggy, and I thought of the first time I'd heard his voice and seen his angelic face. My eyes widened. *Angel* … I thought. *Sorin is my angel after all.*

"I know," I quickly blurted out, and his eyebrows rose as he looked at me. "I know what you are," I said. He was an angel; I convinced myself. His ice-blue eyes, his voice, even his scent. It all relaxed me and helped me find peace. He somehow was exactly what I needed right now. The timing of it was all too perfect. He himself had said that he saved my mother's life years ago. Now he was here trying to save my life, trying to save me from myself. I could no longer support my head, and leaned back against the wall behind me. I sighed. "An angel." I smiled softly. "You're my angel, Sorin." His face showed a mixture of surprise and disgust at my explanation. My heart fell; I was wrong. "But your voice," I moaned. "The way you make me feel. You knew about the pills. Sorin, you knew what I was about to do and stopped me." My eyes quickly teared up. I couldn't be wrong about him.

"You are right, Mia ... I can influence you in many ways, and I did know what you were about to do. I should have confessed it all from the beginning, and I do realize that ... just too late. I will do my best to explain it to you now. First, I am no angel, Mia ... not even close. ..." His voice trailed off.

My arms fell to my sides, and my legs slipped forward in front of me. *The pill!* I screamed to myself, batting at the toilet to my left. I changed my mind. I did not dread the thought of vomiting, after all. Sorin was going to explain everything, and I wasn't about to just pass out now. I lifted my right arm to the cupboard door and pushed off against it. My head bobbed as I tried to lift the lid, but it wouldn't budge.

"Mia," he whispered. "Stop ... it is too late."

My eyes, filled with tears, focused on the lid. Sorin held it down. I hadn't even noticed that he'd moved from the door. "Wh ... why?" My words sounded slurred; I could hardly speak. He'd almost forced me to rid myself of the pill earlier, and yet now he was stopping me.

"It is too late now. The pill is too far into your system. It would be pointless to try to purge yourself of it."

Sorin leaned over and pulled me to him, moving us both to sit against the door. I made a pathetic attempt to crawl back to the toilet. I shoved against him. He nuzzled my face and took a deep breath; he was smelling me again. "I can smell it, the medicine. … You cannot force it out now." He said it so coldly. I whimpered and tried to push him away. "No … you did this, Mia. You chose to do this to yourself. Maybe it will make this easier for both of us."

He would allow the pill to take me away. As punishment for what I'd almost succeeded in doing … had he not interrupted me. Tears finely spilled from my eyes, streaking my cheeks. Sorin's arms wrapped around me, and he pulled me onto his lap. He rested my head on his left shoulder and draped my legs over his thigh. I closed my eyes and felt him lay the towel over me as best he could. I had lost all tension in my body and threatened to fall away from him. Sorin groaned something about suicidal tendencies, and his left arm crossed my back, tightening around my waist. I shuddered as his other hand slid under the towel and cupped my naked thigh. He squeezed it gently, pressing me tighter against him. "Mia … you still with me?" He asked, hopeful. All I could do was nod a yes against him. "You only have a few minutes before the medicine completely claims you. But I promise I will explain all I can until then."

His voice had turned. Now he sounded torn, perhaps even tormented. "I am no angel … But if you are willing to believe me a celestial being, semihuman will not be difficult to grasp." Sorin stopped, squeezing me against his body again. Only this time it felt as if he were trying to comfort himself. "I am a vampire, Mia." He spoke slowly, and his voice was soft. "Not exactly what the current movies and books portray my kind as. But if I were to describe myself and others like me, 'vampire' would be the closest description." I moaned, trying to force out words, but my mouth wouldn't move. He gave a short chuckle and then continued. "I really wish I knew what you were trying to say. Because the colors around you are absolute chaos." I had no idea what he meant. "Some things the movies and books have depicted correctly. If you can still think clearly, reflect on the past few days … I am sure moments will stand out now."

I did as he suggested. I tried to think of all the vampire movies I had watched, comparing them to the past few days we'd spent together. I hadn't seen him in the sunlight or even outdoors, period. He had not eaten anything. The whole strawberry fiasco flooded back. Sorin was pale, but his touch wasn't cold. I tried to lift my left hand to his face, to feel his skin. He misunderstood my intent. His hand let go of my thigh and covered my hand. With a soft fluid movement he tucked our hands under his sweater and against his chest. His skin was cool to the touch. My palm lay gently against his chest, and his hand held mine there. My eyes fluttered open, and I looked down, aware now of where our hands were placed: right over his heart … only I couldn't feel it beating. I tried to talk again, but this time only a pitiful squeak came out. His hand pressed mine harder to his chest. Sorin was right; I had convinced myself he was an angel who had come to take me away. To help me find peace, take me from this earth. But everything was more like a scene from a vampire movie. "I know that it is much to comprehend, Mia … but I am what I say, and I know part of you feels it. You know it is true, and you believe the words I am telling you." Sorin kissed the top of my head and tensed against me. "I swear, the minute you are lost to me for the night I am disposing of those wretched pills … you smell awful." He turned his head away and was quiet.

My temples began to feel as if a tightening vise surrounded my head. My body was sinking, moving farther and farther away from me. It was nothing at all like the way Sorin made me feel. Those soft fades away from reality, drifting into a warm bliss. No this felt like I was being dragged down; it felt heavy, no warm snowflakes now. I wanted that, to hear his seductive voice and melt against him. It took everything I had, but I cleared my throat and spoke. Only it was jumbled and inaudible. "Sis not worm snaflas." I squeezed my eyes tight, frustrated at my failure. *This is not warm snowflakes!* I thought fiercely but didn't bother attempting to say it again.

His body jerked under me, and a half laugh escaped him. "Tomorrow, Mia. … You can tell me all about worms tomorrow." Sorin lowered my hand from his chest and draped it over my lap. His hand slid back under the towel and stopped just above my knee. His head leaned back against the door with a loud thud. "And tomorrow I will explain everything else … and hope you can forgive me." He said the last words with anguish. I couldn't focus anymore, as his voice was starting to sound far away. I wanted to fight it, to stay right here and keep listening. I twitched and sighed. I couldn't fight it any longer.

"*Shh … Shh …* stop fighting it, Mia. … Remember you did this to yourself. It was a choice … accept it." He swayed my body lightly against him, or at least that's what I felt. Before I crashed into darkness, I heard Sorin's voice one more time. Only he wasn't speaking to me. "And I must remember I did this to us. ... All those years ago it was my choice to save your mother. To save your life and forever be tied to you."

I hadn't done the math when he told me how long ago he'd saved my mother, I realized groggily. She was pregnant with me, just out of her first trimester, if I was right. My last thought was of my mother, pregnant, scared, and bleeding. Sorin coming to her rescue, saving both our lives that night.

Chapter 9

Thankfully, I didn't dream that night—or at least didn't remember dreaming come morning. My eyes lifted open and slowly focused. I was looking at a candle, softly glowing, and a glass of water next to it. I looked a little harder and rubbed my eyes. There was a bottle of aspirin next to the candle. My eyes lowered to the nightstand all these objects rested on.

I was upstairs in my bedroom, in my bed. I ran my hand over the sheets, and smooth satin greeted me. I started to stir and lifted my head, only to cringe at the sudden sensation. My head was throbbing. Pressure surrounded it as the sensation grew. I propped myself up on my left elbow, grabbing the aspirin bottle with my right hand. I shook two pills out into my palm, quickly washing them down with the water. As I tilted my head up and swallowed, the previous night flooded back.

All of it—the pills, and Sorin stopping me from ending my life.

Vampire. The word echoed in my head. I turned onto my back and fell against the pillow under me. Had it all been a dream? Or maybe an effect of the pill? The stress of the past week had caused me to blur the lines of reality.

The candle's shadow danced against the ceiling above, and I wondered what time it was. I knew I had slowly slipped into a reversed sleep schedule. Sleeping in all day and not waking up until late afternoon or early evening had become habit. Besides the candle, there wasn't any light in the room, and I guessed it was nightfall or close to it. I lifted my head, looking toward the curtains. I slowly sat up;

something was different about them. They were sheer black with thin intertwining lines embossed on them. Behind the sheers I had hung a dark-wine liner that usually let in a little light. But the closer I looked, I realized light wasn't even coming in from above the window frame.

I pulled back the sheet that covered me back and rose slowly so that my head wouldn't ache even more. I started to the window when the air hit my legs. I was still wearing the little black nightgown from the night before. My face warmed again, just as it had in the bathroom the night before. I stepped to my dresser, which stood between two large windows, and lifted the soft silk over my head. I stood there, naked, looking at the nightgown in utter disgust. I balled it up and tossed it to my left, where it hit the bathroom door and fell to the floor.

I slowly opened and closed multiple dresser drawers, pulling a hunter green ribbed tank top from one and some cotton pajama bottoms from another. Satisfied I was finally wearing something presentable, I went to the window. I reached out and felt the top two layers of curtains, which I moved them aside. With my other hand I felt the window. It was covered with something thick and soft, a blanket maybe. No light came through. I found the edge with my fingers and was about to pull it back.

"Please leave it." Sorin's voice broke the absolute silence that filled the room. I jumped and spun around to the door, but he wasn't there. The door was closed, and my eyes darted around the dimly lit room. "Please leave the curtains closed, Mia. ... At least for another hour, until the sun retires for the night." He sounded at home, at ease.

My eyes followed his voice to the bed, and my heart began to increase its rhythm. He had been in my bed the entire time, tucked under the covers on the opposite side of the mattress. I'd stood here completely nude only moments ago, just a few feet from him. Had he watched, seen my body bare by candlelight? My stomach tightened, and I covered my midsection, trying to ease the knot the way.

"Come back to bed, Mia. I have much to explain … and truly hope you can forgive me for what I have done." Sorin spoke softly, in that alluring tone that drew me in. All my muscles relaxed, and my skin felt warm all over. As always when he used this voice, I did as he asked. My body seemed to float back to the bed. Climbing back under the sheet, I sat with my back to the wall against a pillow. I had become used to this feeling of clouds filling my head. It would pass if Sorin remained quiet for a few minutes. I inhaled a deep breath, one after another, and waited. Looking around my room, knowing the lovely fog would lift soon.

I had missed my room, I realized, as I finally returned to it. I looked around at the deep wine-colored walls and dark cherry-stained wood flooring. Each wall held two or three black cast-iron candleholders on them. They were a gift from my mother for my seventeenth birthday. She had found them at her favorite antique store and teased me about being old enough to have open flames in my room. They were each somewhat unique in their own way. All were black and held one or two candles. But each design twisted and curved differently. The dresser, bed, and nightstands that sat on either side were a black stained wood.

The room was coordinated around my bedding. I had been flipping through a holiday catalog just before my November birthday and saw the bedding set. I had never seen anything like it and had to have it. The sheet set was black satin with a matching dust ruffle. The comforter was wine-colored satin on one side and lush velvet on the reverse. I looked over to the other side of the bed and saw the comforter. I had been storing it in my closet over the summer and simply had not noticed it beside me until that moment. I ran my hand over the top of it. The velvet was soft, and the single candle's flame made it difficult to make out the pattern it held. But the image filled my head from memory: dark red roses on a black background. The decorative pillows were a mix of black velvet and red satin, with a rose design sewn into them. A canopy hung from the ceiling surrounding the bed. My father had built it for me to add curtains to. It had taken a few more months to find the ones I felt were perfect. They were a sheer black, similar to the ones that covered my windows. But they were a heavier fabric with embossed roses in a velvety pattern.

My favorite part of the whole room had been an unexpected discovery. One night I lit all the candles on the walls. Spread out the rose curtains that usually were tied at the four corners of the bed. It was beautiful, the candlelight, when bright enough, made roses appear on the ceiling above me. Shadows of oversized rose shapes danced above on the ceiling as the flames flickered. After the discovery, whenever I had a hectic day, I would escape to my room and recreate that night, watching the ceiling.

I took another look around my room. It had become my escape from the world, and I really had missed it. My head had finally cleared, and I turned back to the heavy comforter that I now knew concealed Sorin. It clicked somewhere in my head—the sweaters he had worn the past few days. Now he lay buried under a velvet comforter. It was how he kept warm. I reached over and slowly eased the comforter down. Sorin lay on his side, a foot or two away from me. He had his back to me, his arms encircling the pillow his head lay on. The candlelight failed to reach the other side of the bed completely. I could make out no details of Sorin in the dim light, just his left shoulder and the side of his face. I couldn't tell if his eyes were open or closed.

"Is your head finally clear Mia?" He sounded amused. He knew exactly what effect he'd had on me when he spoke only minutes before. Sorin even knew a part of me craved it; I had confessed as much.

"Tell me how you do that, how make me fade away." I paused and smiled to myself. "Warm snowflakes," I murmured.

"*Ahh.*" He sounded like he finally understood. "Not 'worm, 'warm.' You were trying to explain warm snowflakes to me last night. I was worried that pill had done some real damage. But now I understand. Is that what it feels like to you? ... I have never heard that description before." He lay there, relaxed in posture, but kept his back to me. I wasn't sure if he thought I didn't want to face him or if there was another reason.

"How do you do it?" I reminded him of my question, my voice a little stern this time.

96

"I already explained it to you. You are simply responding to my voice and what I can offer you. Calm, a sense of peace when you need it." He paused." You yearn for it, no? ... You want my voice, my body to put you at ease. I can only do what you desire of me, Mia. You control me." His voice was soft. Sorin's explanation wasn't easy to understand. He always talked like there might be a second meaning. He seemed to speak in code, or maybe I just didn't know enough about him— "his kind," as he put it—to fully understand. I wanted to see his face, to look into his ice-blue eyes. I had so many questions for him, and I didn't want to have a conversation without him facing me.

I gently placed my hand on his shoulder and turned my body toward him. "Sorin ... look at me." I whispered, afraid of rejection. He kept his body turned away from me; I wasn't sure why. The muscles in his shoulder tensed, and I let my hand fall way.

"I am worried I will frighten you. It may be too much for you." I could hear concern in his voice. But, once again, his words made no sense to me.

Frustrated, my voice came out louder than intended. "You said yourself you have much to explain, and so many questions are swimming through my head, I can hardly focus. I'm beginning to believe it is going to be a long night. I really don't want to spend it conversing with you turned away from me." I winced. I sounded so abrupt and rude. But he stirred, and my heart skipped a beat.

He sat up and gradually turned to face me. "You are right, Mia ... it is going to be a long night." Sorin's words ended just as his eyes met mine.

I gasped, and my hands flew to my mouth. His eyes reflected the candlelight beside me. Similar to a wild animal's caught in the headlights of a car. They were a mixture of pale blue and silver, and they held a slight glow. *They're amazing!* I thought to myself. I didn't mean to, but I had backed away from him.

He appeared a little hurt, and his eyes fell to the bed between us. "I knew it would be too much. I should have warned you." His voice was a mixture of emotions.

Trying to relax, I lowered my hand and placed it on his to show him I wasn't afraid. "Look at me." I couldn't help but feel butterflies inside as he looked back up at my face. His eyes usually were ice blue and seemed to look into my very soul. But now they were absolutely mesmerizing, and I could have sat there forever simply looking into them. I turned my body to face him and moved closer to his side of the bed. "I am sorry if my initial reaction led you to believe I was scared or repulsed. I promise you it's just the opposite. Sorin, I think you're gorgeous, and your eyes right now … I can't even think of words to do them justice. I could get lost in them. They are mesmerizing."

I swallowed hard and tried to keep my voice steady. My breath was slowly quickening, and my heartbeat increased. His head tilted in that odd way I adored more and more each time, and his gaze circled me. This time I realized his eyes weren't circling my face as a normal person's would. No Sorin's eyes were looking around me. Wider than my face, or perhaps seeing someplace else.

"You are not afraid." His voice had a hint of awe and confusion. His eyes traced another circle. "And you are not repulsed in the least." This was one of those moments that felt like there was more to it.

"What is that?" I asked.

He straightened his head and thought for a moment. "What are you questioning, Mia?" He sounded like he knew exactly what I meant but wanted to confirm before continuing. I was having trouble keeping my thoughts focused with his eyes dancing around my body.

"You know what I am asking about. You've done it for days now. ..." My voice trailed off.

"Maybe we should brighten the room before I enlighten you?" His voice held a touch of amusement.

"*Hmm?*" was all I could manage.

Sorin lightly chuckled and looked down at the bed between us again. "You cannot help but feel entranced right now ... so close to me. I imagine between my voice and my eyes, you are struggling to keep your thoughts clear. That is how it should be with us. Without trying, when I speak to you and look at you ... you should feel drawn to me. However, I think it best to illuminate the room further and give you some distance." He reached over and raised my hand to his lips, kissing it.

Sorin let go of my hand, and just as it fell to the bed, more light filled the room from multiple lit candles. I froze and looked at each sconce on the wall. Almost each one now held a burning candle. "Breathe, Mia," he lightly teased.

I blinked and took a deep breath, amazed. I hadn't even seen him move. I looked from the wall to him; as more light now filled the room, I could see his face clearer. His eyes still drew me in slightly. "Again," I said. I couldn't help but be intrigued. "More candles, but slower this time." I wanted to see it again. Like a child watching a magician, trying to figure out the trick.

He reached down from where he stood, suddenly beside me, and tucked a loose curl behind my ear. "Anything you want." Sorin smiled lightly, and his eyes turned a little mischievous. Before I could blink, he was across the room lighting the first candle. He paused at each one and slowly lit it so I could see him. But from candle to candle he was a blur. Gradually the room filled with even more light, and Sorin was back on the bed next to me. I couldn't contain myself. "That was better than the movies!" I blurted out.

He scowled and lines filled his brow. "It is not all like the movies." He spoke with irritation."

But you are really fast," I pointed out, feeling a little giddy.

His face softened, and his head tilted. He was studying me. Sorin grinned and looked pleased. "Your color is improving. ..." His voice trailed off.

My patience had worn thin on his cryptic observations. I smacked the bed below me with both hands. "That is it!" I said in a raised voice. "For days you've looked at me ... like you are observing something. Studying me ... I'm not sure how to explain it. But you just did it. Then there are the cryptic comments, something about my color." I balled my hands into fists and took a deep breath. "I realize now it is not my cheeks you are referring to you." I sighed. "There is so much I want to know, so many questions I want to ask. But if you tilt your head one more time at me ... in that ... way ... I will scream."

Sorin's grin deepened further, and his eyes wandered away. He was thinking. Maybe trying to find the right words, maybe trying to come up with a lie. I could feel my forehead crease, and my eyes narrowed, locking on his. He suddenly looked back at me, right into me as usual.

I felt my shoulders straighten. "Don't lie to me," I said. "I could see you trying to decide … something just now." I lifted my chin a little and raised my eyebrows, as if to challenge him to deny it.

His grin faded away, and he lightly shook his head. "Mia, I could not lie to you even if I wanted to. I have deceived you these past few days. But even when I was not truly honest, you knew." He sounded sincere.

I scoffed. "More cryptic words," I accused. "I don't understand." I lay my head against the wall feeling drained.

His face slowly changed, jaw tightening, and I could see him contemplating something. "Mia, I know you understand so much more than you realize. Your body has responded to me in so many ways since I have been here with you. But I suppose it is all a little too much for your mind to grasp, and with good reason." Sorin paused, and his back stiffened. He looked as if he was preparing himself. But for what I had no idea. He shook his head. "Mia," he forced out, "I have decided I made a terrible mistake coming here. I should not have done so and feel I should leave immediately!" His words sounded forced and rehearsed.

Just as the confusion started to fill me, my mouth filled with saliva. A horrible wave of nausea came over me, and my stomach started turning. I gagged, my hands flew to my mouth, and I started to scramble off the bed. Sorin caught me, and his arm wrapped around my waist, pulling me to him. His other arm locked around my chest. "Let me go!" I yelled into my hand. "I'm about to be sick." I gagged as another wave of nausea washed over me. His arms were locked tight around me as I looked over to my bathroom door. My back was pressed against his chest as I sat between his legs. "They were lies. Everything I just said—all lies. You can taste them." He stilled momentarily. "It would be pointless for me to lie to you. You would taste my deception every time." He said it so matter-of-factly.

I stopped struggling against him. The taste in my mouth was bitter, medicinal. Like the times before. My mind went back to all the times I had experienced it. It had never been this strong. First I'd thought it was the tea, and then I had accused him of putting something in my food.

"Just relax. ... It will pass," he softly whispered, and his arms loosened their hold. I lay my head back against him and let my arms fall to my stomach. Was it unimaginable, the thought of being able to taste someone's lies? My stomach began to calm, and I thought maybe a part of me had almost figured it out. I remembered seeing an episode of medical mysteries on the science channel. The first story was about a young blind boy. But, like a bat or dolphin, he could click his tongue and use sonar to get around. I recalled the second story now—a pair of sisters who could taste words. The disorder was called synesthesia. Each word tasted different to them. Or maybe each word had a color. It had been so long, I couldn't remember the details. I'd thought it was amazing at the time. But now, experiencing something similar, I felt sorry for them. I took a few deep breaths and tried to believe everything that was happening.

Sorin explained that almost all vampires experienced different degrees of the disease. And it was believed that it had been passed down through the blood.

"Promise you'll never lie to me again, Sorin." I pleaded, hoping I would never experience that again. My temple rested against his cheek, and I felt the muscles change. He was smiling, but just a little.

He spoke, and it was a light and genuine. "I will never so boldly lie to you again, Mia; as I just showed, you any attempt would be futile." Sorin's arms released me completely, and each of his hands descended to rest over mine. The bitter taste was finally fading from my mouth.

His words sank in, and they had an all-too-familiar hidden meaning. I blinked, trying to get my thoughts together. I sat up and moved away from him. Sorin stayed where he was, leaning his left shoulder against the wall, his eyes drinking me in. "So boldly lie?" I repeated his words as a question.

He looked slightly surprised to see I had caught that there was more to his words. "You could lie to yourself if you truly wanted to. A lie is simply someone's perception or desire of what they really want. We could look at the same starry sky. I could say how filled with stars the night sky is. When you look up and only see a few. Which is a lie?" Sorin shrugged his shoulders, running his fingers through his hair. "It is all in one's perception. ... Maybe I simply see more stars than you. I will never purposefully lie to you. But I cannot promise that our perceptions on subjects are even close currently." His eyes surveyed me, and I felt my body tense when he said it. "You look like you are feeling better though, your—"

I cut him off before he could finish. "Your color looks much better." I spat at him, annoyed. "Explain it."

He nodded. "Just as it is obvious to you when I lie ... your emotions are obvious to me. Color surrounds you, Mia. It radiates from your body; it changes as your mood or feelings change. Not just you; all humans have colors around them."

I thought about it for a minute, imagined it was someone's aura he could see. After just experiencing been able to taste his lies, his seeing my mood wasn't a far stretch. I tried to picture it in my head, but it was a struggle. "Explain it to me. Describe which colors you see. ... Please." I slipped down under the sheet and lay on my side, facing Sorin. I tucked a pillow under my head and waited.

I watched as his face slowly changed. Sadness filled his eyes. "Every one of your kind is different. Some of the colors are bright, vivid. Some have dark clouds around them." His voice ached. Sorin reached down, and his hand cupped the side of my face. "You have only darkness around you Mia. You have been surrounded by the colors of death and sorrow. It has lessened, but not to a great extent." His voice made my eyes water. I could hear how hard it had been for him to look at me and see my pain for days now. His thumb caressed my cheek, and I closed my eyes briefly. He continued. "Each emotion has its own color, and a human can be surrounded by more than one color. Just as a human can feel more than one emotion at a time." I closed my eyes and pictured it, a soft cloud that surrounded me. My stomach knotted a little. The air around me sounded colorless, black. I opened my eyes and looked up at Sorin. His expression hadn't changed.

I tried to lighten the mood. "I imagine it's beautiful, the colors you see. I loved it when new crayon colors were created as a child. When I paint I love mixing colors and creating new ones." I thought for a moment. "You said every emotion has a color. … What color is joy?" I wanted to try imagining what he saw when he looked at humans when they were happy. His hand left my cheek and he laid it over mine where it rested on the bed between us.

Sorin's face lightened, and his eyes drifted away for a minute. "Your kind is so complicated when it comes to emotions. It is like fingerprints." He paused and looked down at our hands. He turned my hand over and traced the lines in my palm with his finger. His fingers spread out and covered each of mine. "Yellow is usually the color that surrounds the joyful. But the shades of yellow are endless. It is never the same color of joy for two people. Maybe a human is happy and excited, or in high spirits and nervous." He half smiled. "Picture the largest box of crayons you had when you were young. Then imagine each one of those crayons and the possible shades, darker or lighter."

I closed my eyes and saw my favorite color when I was little. "My favorite color was cerulean." I whispered to myself. I imagined the blue color a single shade lighter, then even lighter. I pictured it a shade darker, and then even darker.

Sorin must have guessed what was going through my head. "Now imagine that crayon and all its possibilities mixed with all the other crayon colors." His voice slowly trailed in the distance as a world of colors swam through my head.

Eventually I opened my eyes and looked at Sorin. "It sounds breathtaking." My voice filled with awe.

His lips tightened. "To you, yes. I am sure you would view it as beautiful. It usually is. ... But along with the beautiful emotions—joy, love, compassion—come very ugly ones. Even after all these years, it is still hard to see the dark colors around humans. To see them surrounded by the colors of greed, deception, and hate. I welcome my life of solitude." He glanced around the room. "It is over stimulating at times, Mia. Easily hearing everyone's conversations all at once, seeing all the colors. But after a while, a dark room and silence are all I desire."

His words pulled at my heart. My eyes drifted to his sweater, a dark gray. Just a shade or two lighter than yesterday's. I reached out and felt the bottom of his sleeve. It was even softer than it looked. "You have worn nothing but dark clothes since you've been here, and always sweaters."

A smile gently played across his lips. Sorin looked at me and then over to my closet. His smile deepened a little. "I am not the only one who has a wardrobe absent of color." An eyebrow rose slightly, and his expression was one of teasing.

I wasn't sure what he meant. I shrugged at him. "What are you talking about?" I asked.

Sorin nodded his head toward my closet. "Have you never noticed what lack of color your closet holds?" He looked down at the bed and then around the room. "Even your room is predominantly in black. The only color is a deep wine."

I felt my face warm at the thought of his being in my bedroom, seeing my things. I looked at my closet door, trying to think of everything it enclosed. "I only went into your closet for the comforter. I apologize, but it was necessary. I could not help but notice the lack of bright colors in your closet."

I wrinkled my nose at him. "We can't all be sunbeams and rainbows, Sorin." I shrugged and explained further. "Other than my painting, colors don't appeal to me. I don't wear all black … just dark, rich colors." I looked around my room. "The thought of a bright-yellow or bubblegum-pink bedroom makes my stomach turn."

He looked toward the window and down to me. "The sun is down. …. How does some fresh air sound?"

His hand gently squeezed mine.

Chapter 10

Sorin pulled the covers away, and in a single breath, darkness filled the room. He had put out all the candles and was opening my bedroom door. A light chuckle escaped me as I pulled the sheet back. I walked around the bed and joined him by the door. He smiled lightly, offering his arm. I cupped my hand over the inside of his elbow, and he led me down the hall.

I stopped at the top of the stairs and looked back down the hallway. I hadn't noticed it the night before, but all the pictures had been removed. Empty nails lined the wall. I looked to Sorin, but he answered my question before I could even ask it. "I removed them from the table for you. After your physical response to them that first day, I thought it best not to hang them just yet." He paused. "Mia, if you want them back on the walls, I will return them." His free hand cradled my cheek, and he kissed my forehead. "I am only trying to make it a little more bearable for you, anyway I can."

My eyes watered. I thought Jenny had cleared them from the table and returned them to the walls. "Thank you," I whispered.

He walked me to the kitchen and pulled my usual stool out for me. "You should eat before we go outside. What sounds appealing?" He turned and opened the refrigerator. "More strawberries?" he asked, and I heard the container crinkle in his hand. "Actually, the strawberries smell a little ... overripe." Sorin threw them away and returned to the fridge. A few things were shuffled around. "I think you should choose what to eat." He passed my side and sat on the stool across from me, looking apologetic. "I forgot how awful food can smell sometimes. Some of that has expired and should be removed."

He was right. I hadn't cleaned out the fridge since the accident. It was something my mother usually took care of. I crossed my arms over one another on the counter in front of me and laid my head on them. "I don't want to eat." I felt like crying yet again. He reached out and squeezed my shoulder. The silence was broken when my stomach growled. I knew he heard it. I quickly lifted my head and glared at him—a warning to keep silent.

He lightly chuckled, understanding my meaning, which he chose to ignore. "How about a banana and some crackers?" His voice had a slightly pleading tone.

"I give up," I mumbled. "Whatever. ... Nothing sounds good to me, Sorin. I'm going to go outside for some fresh air. I will eat later." I slipped off the stool and headed down the hall to the patio door.

By the time I was sliding the door open Sorin was behind me. Food filled one of his arms, and he had a glass of juice in the other. I couldn't hold back a small smile. I wondered if I would ever get used to his moving so quickly. I opened the patio door and the outdoor lights automatically flicked on. I sat at the outdoor table and watched as he placed all the food in front of me. The glass of juice looked refreshing, but I waited for him to set everything down. He had raided the pantry in the time it took me to walk down the hallway. He placed a box of crackers before me. And a bag of pistachios, followed by a granola bar, and, last of all, a banana that had just started to spot from age.

I laughed lightly. "I cannot eat all of this … but I will eat something." I drank some juice and nibbled on the crackers. Sorin sat back in his chair and admired the night sky. I followed his gaze and took a deep breath. It was warm out, and I could smell the humidity in the air. We just sat there in silence as I slowly ate.

I reached for the bag of pistachios, but his hand caught mine as I pulled the bag toward me. A sly look crept over his face. "Allow me, Mia," he offered. I opened my mouth to protest but stopped. I looked down, and his palm already held a handful of shelled nuts. He emptied the shelled nuts into my palm. "It has been difficult to slow my movements," he admitted. "I did slip once or twice … but I believe it went unnoticed." He looked a little smug.

I finished the glass of juice and noticed that the air had become cooler. Sorin's chin lifted, and he looked off into the distance. "We should head inside. It will rain soon." His voice had its usual confidence. He stood up slowly, and I pushed my chair from the table. I picked up the empty glass and reached for everything else, but it was gone. I turned to the patio door behind me. Sorin stood in front of the patio door waiting for me, with food and empty wrappers in hand.

"Now you're just showing off." I put my free hand on my hip.

His head tilted just a little and his eyes circled to me. "But a part of you enjoys it every time, Mia." He said it with such assurance that I didn't bother to argue with him. He went inside, and I followed, locking the door behind me. I paused; the act of locking the door to keep out intruders suddenly seemed silly. I was actually locking myself inside with the most dangerous person I knew.

Questions quickly filled my head. I knew so little about Sorin. Everything he had shared with me during the past few days had been partial truths. I wanted to know it all—the true interaction he'd had with my mother years ago. I walked to the kitchen and stopped in the doorway. Sorin sat on his stool. I looked at him, seeing an absolutely beautiful man before me. His skin looked so light next to his dark hair, and his eyes were a shade of blue I had never seen before. How had I not noticed his true appearance before? It made me feel oblivious to what had been right in front of me. The way he looked, the way he looked at me. Even the way he was dressed was so different.

I leaned against the doorway frame, and scenes from my favorite vampire movies flashed through my head. Scenes of blood, gore, murder. I swallowed as visions of passion and seduction raced through my thoughts. Maybe that was why I hadn't seen it before; I wasn't supposed to. My mind raced through details about Sorin. He never ate, always made excuses, but forced me to eat. Overdressed for the weather, and yet he still felt cool to the touch. Sunlight hadn't been an issue, as I had hardly seen it myself lately. I was supposed to be drawn in by him, falling at his feet and baring my neck to him. That's how it was in the movies. The night before, I had gone to his room to seduce him, only he wasn't there. I'd thought he'd left without a word, and then I'd taken the sleeping pill ... tried to take even more. And then he'd saved me. My stomach knotted up. How much did the movies have accurate—none of it, all of it, or somewhere in between?

I pushed myself from the doorway and crossed to the sink, setting the juice glass in it. I turned to Sorin, leaning against the sink with my arms crossed. I bit my lip, trying to decide where to begin, what to ask first. Sorin's eyes traced me and then locked on mine.

His face was somber. "I no longer have any secrets from you, Mia. ... Ask." He waited, sitting perfectly still.

The truth was, I didn't know where to start. "I loved scary movies growing up ... Frankenstein, witches, werewolves ... but vampire movies were my favorite. I watched them all." I fell silent, searching for my next words. "I am suddenly wondering how much of the movies I have watched all these years were accurate." His mouth began to move, and he looked like he was about to say something, but then he stopped himself. "I think if I were simply a meal to you ... I would be dead by now." I winced. I had said it so flippantly. "If it was ... seduction ... or intimacy. ..." I struggled for the words. Closing my eyes, I rubbed my right temple, which had started to ache. "I'm just wondering, in light of the recent revelation, why you're here ... with me." I let my arms drop to my sides and looked over at him, eager for his response.

"I am here for *you,* Mia." His eyes fell to the counter in front of him. "I came to you with the hope of easing some of your agony, to console you if allowed." He sat there, again still and silent. He had comforted me multiple times these past few days, had become a welcome distraction.

112

Thunder boomed overhead, and I jumped, my heart racing. My hands flew to my chest, and I gasped. I looked up at the ceiling and then at Sorin, and I froze. His eyes were wild and his nostrils were slightly flared. My eyes descended to his mouth, his jaw flexed so tight, every muscle showed. Sorin's hands clenched the edge of the marble counter in front of him. I felt my heart pounding under my palm and slowly considered the possibilities. Could he hear my heart's assault against my chest? Did I smell of fear suddenly? Whatever it was, my response to the sudden thunder triggered something in him. I felt locked in his gaze, and my head started to feel light. My body tingled, and my eyes felt heavy, slowly closing. I imagined him slowly slipping from his seat and crossing the kitchen floor to my side. His eyes devouring me as one of his hands wrapped around my waist, roughly pressing me against him. His other hand creeping up my arm and pausing on the side of my neck. My mouth felt dry, and my breath started to quicken; the vision continued. His thumb pressing just below my jaw, feeling my pulse race. His hands lifting away, fingers intertwining in my hair and gently tilting my head to the side. I couldn't help but whimper a little.

"Mia!" Sorin rasped, and my eyes shot open. He hadn't moved, still sat with his hands clinging to the edge of the counter. His eyes were closed, and lines filled his forehead. "Leave the room … please."

My body quiver at the sound of his voice begging me to leave his side. I could hear the warning in his voice too. My feet wouldn't move at first. I stumbled to the wall and followed it to the dining room. I paused, clinging to one of the chairs and trying to clear my head. I thought of his hands on my body, on my neck as he tilted my head back. I wondered how it would feel to have Sorin's mouth on my neck. I turned, taking a single step back to the kitchen. A part of me considered returning to him.

"Mia!" he roared. "Keep going!" Any restraint had left his voice, sending chills up my spine.

I crossed the foyer and sat down on the sofa. I tucked myself into the corner and pulled a blanket to my lap. I wasn't cold, but I held it as a form of protection. I stared past the doorway, wondering when Sorin would join me. Minutes passed, and the thunder stopped. My heartbeat returned to normal as I calmly waited. I swallowed, and my throat was dry. A thought crossed my mind. "I'm really thirsty," I whispered as low as I could to myself. I watched the foyer, curious. Just as I wondered if my assumption was correct, he entered, a glass of water in his hand.

I fought a grin and reached out for the glass. Sorin handed it to me and swiftly returned to the doorway. He started to pace slowly, not looking at me once. I drank the water and placed the glass on a nearby coffee table. I decided to break the silence. "Sorin?" I whispered. He stopped pacing, but kept his eyes on the floor before him. "Can you hear my heartbeat from across the room?" I spoke in a hushed tone again, waiting for his answer. He simply nodded yes. I continued whispering. "Can you smell my blood from where you stand?" I bit my lip after the words left me. I remembered how he had smelled me after I'd taken the sleeping pill. Sorin's hands balled into fists at his side, and I had my answer. I began to wonder how hard the previous days had been for him. He had been gentle, caring, and compassionate most of the time.

"Come sit down. ... Please." My voice was quiet but no longer a whisper. I was feeling remarkably calm. One last clap of thunder sounded far off, but I didn't respond. I took a deep breath and slowly blew it past my lips. Sorin leisurely came to the sofa and sat in the opposite corner. As far away from me as he could place himself. "Some of what I have seen in the movies is true about vampires." It was a statement, something to fill the hollow air between us.

"Your books, movies, and television have many incorrect qualities of my kind. Each one slowly creeps farther away from any reality I know." Sorin massaged his forehead and let his arm fall across his thigh. "If you want answers ... simply ask me, Mia." He finally looked at me, his face full of emotions. Frustration mostly, upset about what had transpired in the kitchen, I safely assumed.

"I would ask you to explain what just happened in there." I motioned to the kitchen. "But ... I think I understand most of it." I sighed, propping my elbow on the back of the sofa and leaning my head against my fist. He sat in front of me, still torturing himself. I recalled the times he tried to distract me with trivial questions. "Garlic?" I asked lightly. It worked. He let go of whatever he was thinking, and a look of confusion crossed his face. "Are you allergic to or have an aversion to garlic?" I asked.

A light smile played on his mouth, and he relaxed into the cushions around him. "What does garlic smell like to you?" His eyebrows rose.

I thought about it for a minute. "Strong, sharp, overpowering." I shrugged.

His smile deepened. "Now imagine what you smell, only a hundred times more intense. Would you mind it then?"

It made sense. The heightened sensitivity. "Oh! ... I hadn't thought about it like that." I thought of other foods. "So, onions, peppers ..." My voice trailed off.

He nodded. "Your food, in general, is an assault on my sense of smell. But garlic will not kill me." I searched for my next question and couldn't help but smile. "Bats?" I chimed, but I had guessed the answer already.

Sorin's smile faded. Which caused mine to end. "Bats are bats, Mia. ... They have nothing to do with me. The fact that some of the movies actually portray vampires with the ability to transform themselves into bats is utterly absurd." He spoke with disgust, and his voice made me shrink back a little.

I tried to smooth things over again. "But you are really fast." He agreed with a soft yes. "And the movies have the acute sense of hearing and smell correct," I persisted. He nodded a yes. "How long have you been dead?" I hoped it wasn't too personal a question. His eyes grew large momentarily, and his body tensed. I cringed inside. I had said something wrong. Was age a sensitive subject, after all?

Sorin gathered himself and proceeded to talk slowly and with much restraint. "If I were ... dead I would be in the ground." He took a moment before explaining further. "I am not dead; I simply age much more slowly than your kind does."

I was a little confused. I remembered his holding my hand over his chest; I'd felt no heart beating beneath my palm. "But I felt your chest. … There wasn't a heartbeat." Had I been wrong? Maybe the pill had really dulled my senses by then.

"Every living creature has an average number of heartbeats." His eyes lowered to my chest. "If you live to the age of eighty years, your heart would have beat over three billion times. I have the same number of heartbeats in my lifetime. Only my heart beats a handful of times an hour, compared to your thirty-six hundred. It beats so slowly, a human could not possibly feel it. I am not dead, Mia; I just age much more slowly." He finally seemed relaxed, so I decided against asking Sorin his true age.

The vision of us filled my thoughts again. Him slowly tilting my head, exposing my neck. "If you were to … bite someone, would they become like you?" The process of becoming a vampire had a wide range of portrayals in the movies.

He tried not to show it, but I could see the question made him a little uneasy. "If all we had to do was bite to turn your kind … I imagine the majority of the population would be vampires by now." He stopped, not going into further detail.

I had that familiar feeling he was holding something back. "So how is it done?" I pressed.

Sorin eyes shifted to a place somewhere above my head. He was struggling to find the correct words. Or trying to decide how much to share. "My kind does need blood to survive … human blood. When we drink a human's blood we take a part of them it into us. That act alone does not turn

117

them." He shifted slightly, continuing to avoid my gaze. "But if I were to share my blood with that same human a bond would be formed." His voice lowered a little. "We would be forever united."

It took a few minutes to try to understand the complexity of it. It sounded intense. "So you drink someone's blood, and vice versa, and then they become like you." I said it as if it were a passing thought. Only his body language and the fact that he still hadn't looked in my direction made me feel I was overlooking something. He was holding back. "Sorin? ...What aren't you telling me?" I sat up and put my hands in my lap.

Slowly his eyes met mine. "It is not that simple, Mia." Thoughts crossed his face as he proceeded cautiously. "When you are intimate ... with a man ... you are giving a part of yourself to him forever." My cheeks flushed under his gaze, yet again. "For humans, it is a form of uniting ... a way of giving themselves to one another. Although times have changed drastically when it comes to this part of their lives, most humans are still selective, careful not to give themselves so freely in an intimate way. It is similar for us ... but out of necessity. The sharing of blood is even more intimate for us— we actually give away a part of ourselves." His eyes slowly glazed over as they drifted to my lap. "My kind would have to drink in a human's blood and then share theirs. Only then would a part of us flow through the human's veins. A part of you feels lost after that. You feel empty or incomplete." His eyes stayed blank, like he was in a trance. "The more blood you share with one another, the more united you become. Eventually the human's heart slows, and the body goes through many … changes." His eyes at last focused on me. "It only takes once for my kind Mia. … Giving my blood one time was enough to change everything. I should not have intervened … I know that now. But I could not simply turn my back on her."

My eyes watered; he was referring to my mother. He had saved her life—my life—all those years ago. Now the reality of it all sank in. Days ago, when he'd first told me the events of that night, he had left out so much. "Tell me about that night again. What really happened, Sorin?" My voice cracked as I wiped away a tear. I didn't really want to hear the whole story and all the details. But I had to know the rest of it. More tears filled my eyes, and I wrapped my arms around my midsection. "Just the parts you left out … please." I hardly recognized my own voice; it was hollow and weak. Sorin shifted slightly, and doubt filled his face. "Please," I repeated.

He reluctantly agreed. "Most of what I told you was true. I was walking at night not far from your mother's shop. I heard your mother scream, and I rushed to the alley … to her side. The man had already injured Jennifer, who lay there unconscious. But I clearly heard a healthy heartbeat. The man had just stabbed your mother and was struggling with her over a bag." He paused. "He took the money and ran. I let him go at that time. … But he did not live to see another sunrise, Mia. I even returned the day's receipts to the shop."

Sorin had just freely admitted to killing the man. I squeezed myself tighter. I should've been repulsed, but a part of me found comfort in the confession. He tried to rush past the gory details, his words spilling out. "Your mother was losing blood, but not too quickly. ... I was sure someone had heard her scream, and called for help. I could have just turned around and left. She probably would have survived. But I took one look at her and knew she was with child." Tears spilled from my eyes, but I sat quiet and listened. "Pregnant women have a color around them that is unmistakable, Mia ... a prism of colors. It is like looking into an opal. The colors constantly change, it is breathtaking." He stopped, and I could see him remembering that moment. "But the utter fear that surrounded her—it was like nothing I had seen before." His voice lowered. "Then she begged me, Mia ... to save her ... to save you." He raked his fingers through his hair. "She was somehow calm in that moment. She held her stomach and talked to you. Kept repeating she would not lose you. Telling you help would arrive soon and to be strong. She looked right at me and said she could not bear the thought of living without you."

His eyes darted away, his voice raised. "It is not my place to decide if a human lives or dies in a moment like that. I should not have altered the outcome. I truly believe she would have lived. ... But you would have been lost, Mia. I have killed men before, but I could not be responsible for the death of a child. It was within my power to save you." He shook his head. "I should not have prolonged my purpose for being out that night. I was following him, had been for a while as he walked around town. I could see he was dishonest and selfish—the very reason I did not feel guilty for what I was about to do. When he turned down the alley I delayed the climax of the hunt. If I had not done so ... your life would not have been in danger of ending. You mother would not have been in peril if had fed on him earlier. I was responsible for your life being at risk and the injuries to your mother. So I did what she asked without a second thought. …" Sorin's gaze locked onto a corner of the room. But the fingers from his right hand lightly touched the opposite wrist. I couldn't see anything from where I sat. "I gave my blood … to save her child." His voice was torn, contrite.

I cleared my throat and wiped away my tears before speaking. "Sorin … was it so awful to save me?" I asked.

His eyes quickly met mine, and I easily saw the anguish that filled them. My heart ached for him, for whatever it was that tore at him. "I gave my blood, Mia … for the first time since I had been turned. My blood flowed through her veins, through yours." His voice started to sound strained. My expression must have shown a lack of understanding about what he was trying to express. "I freely gave myself Mia and only hurt myself in return. A partial bond was made that night … so many years ago. I was drawn to her after that. A part of me desired to take her from here and complete that bond. It is an instinct that takes over and consumes you. To in exchange take a part of that person you just shared yourself with." His eyes glazed over again. "It would be impossible to describe what it does to you … to smell your own blood flowing through someone else's body. I wanted to take her, Mia … I could have tasted her blood right there, without her consent. I could not believe how strong the urge was, enough for me to consider it." His voice lowered to a whisper. "It would have been wrong. I know that … but it does happen." He blinked finally and looked at me. "I left her once I heard the ambulance approaching. I went after the man who had attacked her and Jennifer. I watched her for a few days. Then I put an ocean between us. That was how far I had to be to fight the pull I felt to her. But I was still a part of her ... of you." Sorin's eyes fell to a place between us on the sofa. "When your partner died years ago ... I felt it, Mia. I did not know the cause then as I do now. But I felt your pain, your sorrow. I had to resist the impulse to return to you then. Last week when your mother ... it was not a quick death."

I started sobbing. Unlike my father, I knew she had survived the accident. But I had convinced myself she wasn't in any pain. To hear Sorin say it had been otherwise shattered any composure I had left. Deep down I had known it was the reality but never wanted to believe it. I thought of the fear she must have felt. Maybe even been aware of my father's death. I closed my eyes and buried my face in my hands, crying. Sorin voice was off in the distance. "A part of me died with her, Mia. ... But I could feel your pain ... and I could not stay away this time."

Sorin's words slowly sank in. I moved to his side of the couch and buried my face in his chest. His arms wrapped around me and held me tight. "Please," I begged. "Please make me fade away." I cried into his sweater.

His arms tightened around me. "Are you sure, Mia?" He forced out. "I want to—I will—if it is what you really want. But maybe I am only complicating things by doing so." He sounded so concerned for me.

All I knew at that moment was that I wanted this pain to stop. If he refused to help me, well ... I could end it myself in another way. I pictured the knife near the cutting board in the kitchen, liquor in the cabinet, pain reliever in my bathroom. "Please, Sorin!" I rasped.

His hands smoothed the top of my head, and his arms loosened around me. "Hush … it will be all right. … It will pass. I promise." His voice changed slowly. "I am torn between relieving you of your grief and feeling it is a necessary process." Sorin's tone slowed, began to flow over me. "Take a deep breath." I obeyed. "Now let it out slowly." His voice seeped into me. I obeyed again, blowing the breath past my lips. "Imagine your warm snowflakes, Mia. Keep breathing; let the pain melt away."

After a bit, my head finally turned fuzzy, my body lightened, and the tears slowed. I smelled sandalwood and let myself drift away.

Chapter 11

I must have fallen asleep, because when my eyes opened, I was looking at the family room wall. I blinked and started to stir.

"Slowly, Mia." Sorin's voice purred above me.

"How long did I sleep?" I asked, groggy.

"Just over two hours. .... Your body needed to rest." He slowly lifted me from his lap.

"I feel like all I do is sleep. ... But all I want to do is sleep." I brushed some loose hairs back from my face and sat up.

His beautiful ice-blue eyes looked into mine as he raised my chin. "A little better?" he asked. "I know it was a lot to hear. ... I am sorry." He let go of my chin. "Should we retire for the night? ... I will carry you to bed if you wish."

His voice had lost some of its effect. I couldn't imagine any more deep conversation tonight. I nodded, and in a single fluid movement I was in his arms. In the next instant we were ascending the stairs. I wrapped my arms around his neck and lay my head on his shoulder. I hardly felt each step under us. He turned the light on once in the bedroom and sat me on the edge of the bed. "I am going to the kitchen for you. ... How about an apple?" he asked.

I frowned and waved him away. I looked down at myself and crossed to my bathroom. While brushing my teeth I decided a shower would feel good. But I realized that my shampoo and body wash were still in the guest bathroom downstairs. Kayla had retrieved them for me, along with the black dress and heels. I wondered how good Sorin's hearing actually was. "Could you bring me the bottles from the guest room shower down there, please?" I didn't whisper this time, but I didn't raise my voice either. I pulled some deep-teal satin pajama bottoms from my dresser and a fresh tank top. I was taking my clothes to the bathroom when Sorin walked through my bedroom door. I stopped and turned toward him. I wasn't surprised to see a crisp green apple and a bottle of water in one hand, and my shampoo and body wash in the other. I lightly smiled, holding out my free hand. He passed the toiletries to me and then turned toward the nightstand beside my bed.

I took a long shower, enjoying the water falling on me. I quickly dried off, dressed, and shut off the bathroom light. Starting toward the bed, I halted at the sight before me. Sorin was under the comforter on the side closest to the door. Pillows piled under his head propped him up at an angle. He looked relaxed, one arm bent and tucked under the back of his head. On my nightstand were an apple, a bottle of water, and a small vase of roses from the garden. I looked back at Sorin. This should have made me uncomfortable. A man whom I'd met just a few short days ago was now lying in my bed. But he was more than a man; he was a vampire. And that was what really bothered me inside. As absurd as this moment and scene before me was, I was about to crawl into bed next to him. My response to his existence was abnormal. I should have felt something. Been apprehensive, nervous— or, at the very least, afraid for my life.

And yet, standing there looking at him, not one of those emotions ran through my body. I realized how truly numb I had become. Besides the waves of pain and grief I allowed myself to feel occasionally I had become indifferent toward life. I really did not fear the thought of Sorin draining my blood and my not waking to see tomorrow. The more I stood there and thought about it—envisioned it—the more a part of me welcomed the possibility.

But he had stopped me from taking the pills the other night. Yelled at me earlier during the storm to leave the kitchen, feeling it was for my safety. He didn't want me dead or hurt. Sorin's words earlier had described that my pain would be his to endure. My hopes of not waking up in the morning were fleeting.

Sorin raised his head slightly from the pillow and looked at me, eyes narrowing. "This is new." He said it more to himself than me.

On instinct I started to look down at the clothes I wore but then understood his meaning. I frowned, trying to show my annoyance for his repetitive observations.

"What is it?" he pondered, curious.

I straightened my back and crossed my arms. "I don't know, Sorin." I complained. "What does it look like to you?" I was gradually feeling more irritated by the minute.

His expression faded, and he lay his head back on the pillow and looked at the ceiling above him. His voice was quiet, empty. "Anything other than shades of black and gray is new on you. Anything different, even for only a moment, gives me hope."

My shoulders fell, and I sighed, suddenly feeling impolite. Yet again, I felt not myself. "I was only trying to understand your colors, Mia. It is all I am ever trying to do. I am sorry if I was wrong to ask. …. I will try to refrain next time." The more he spoke, the worse I felt.

When he talked about seeing a human's emotions in colors I had thought it a beautiful sight. Now the thought that I wore my feelings with no control over expressing them made me lose the awe and wonder I'd initially had in response to his description. Maybe it was because I was the human currently being observed. Or perhaps being described as colorless somehow managed to depress me further. Whatever it was, my opinion had definitely changed on the subject.

"I'm sorry, Sorin." My words sounded forced as he lifted his head and looked at me. "I was thinking how unrealistic this is." I tried to think of how to describe it to him. "I'm guessing this whole situation is lost on you. But for me, this moment is absurd. This …" I made a horizontal circle in the air between us. "This is that scene in movies that always seems ridiculous. Where a man and a woman met only days before … and yet they act like they have known each other for years. Somehow there is this magical connection, and they each suddenly know what the other is thinking and feeling. It's all late-night dinners followed by candlelight and soft music as they. …" My voice slowly became louder and more aggravated. "You don't know me, Sorin. … I don't know you. … And yet, I have welcomed you into my home. Right now you are even lying in my bed as if it is completely natural for you." I crossed my arms, waiting for his response.

He sat up and pressed his hands into the mattress on either side of him. Sorin looked down at the bed and then up to me, his face taking on an innocent expression. "This is the only bed that I have laid in since arriving here." It wasn't a confession but an action he had repeated for days now without the slightest regard for my personal space or guest etiquette. He had seen nothing wrong with it.

My jaw went lax. "What?" I whispered in shock.

His expression turned to frustration, but I could see him try to hide it. Sorin leaned forward and patted the bed in front of him. "Come ... here ... Mia." His voice was low and alluring. He was looking at me in a way that made me feel exposed, bare. His eyes did not move from mine. When I failed to advance, his eyes sparkled a little, and he repeated his words. "Come here." His voice warmed my skin and made my body tingle.

I did as he asked. A part of me screamed how wrong it was with every step I took to his side. I paused at the foot of the bed, my head light. Reliving that all-too-familiar marionette sensation somewhere inside me. Sorin slowly lifted his hand from the bed in front of him and held it out for me to take. My body moved on its own. I reached out, taking his hand as he guided me to the empty place on the bed, near his legs. I tucked my feet to my side, against my body. His eyes finally drifted from mine, but only a few inches. I licked my lips, head still light and fuzzy. Sorin let go of my hand and gently cupped my chin. I blinked slowly and then swallowed, my throat suddenly dry. His face crept to mine, and my eyes closed. His cheek brushed mine, and his lips grazed my ear. "You are wrong, Mia," he eventually offered.

My head swam, and I reminded myself to breath. His scent filled my nose, and I was completely hypnotized before him. "Does this really feel absurd to you?" He spoke slowly, letting each word dance in my ear. I could not speak. All I could do was shake my head no. "Do you feel as if you are next to a stranger?" I shook my head again. I felt him softly smile against my cheek. "Do you know why that is?" I blinked, trying to concentrate, trying to think of more than a single-word response. "No" I said weakly, failing in my attempt. Sorin sat back and looked deep into my eyes. "Because you do know me. … You have known me your whole life." His eyes held mine. "On that night I made a choice. … You will forever hold a part of me as a result of that choice." A beautiful grin touched his lips, and his eyes smiled. "And I know you, Mia … I feel what you feel. My instinct is to be at your side. To protect you."

His voice gradually eased back to normal. "We are part of one another. … We are not strangers. If you would only stop fighting it, you could feel everything I do." The clouds were slowly lifting from my head. Sorin's smile faded to a light frown. "All you are doing is fighting right now. The idea of what could be between us. … You fight the wonderful memories you have of your parents until they flood back and overwhelm you." His frown deepened. "You have even fought the desire to live. I have felt this at its peak. As you cut the lemon in the kitchen." The sadness in his voice cleared any lingering cobwebs. "Tell me you will try, Mia … Try to embrace me and all that I have to offer. Beginning with some real peace, not fleeting numbness." Sorin's hand left my face, and he sat back against the wall at the head of the bed.

I stayed in the middle, his words repeating themselves inside my head. Everything he had said was true. From the moment I first heard his voice and saw his face, a sense of peace touched me. I did feel comfortable near him, even in that moment sitting in my bed next to him. When I gave in, he could ease the pain I felt. Looking at him did make a part of me wonder what the next day would bring. I felt like I had lost myself. I looked in the mirror and wondered who I had become. Maybe what Sorin offered could help me find myself.

His eyes drifted past me briefly. "Are you tired?" he asked. I felt drained, exhausted. I always did after our conversations. The thought of lying in bed did appeal to me. I yawned, raising a hand to cover my mouth. He pulled back the covers, inviting me to join him.

I scoffed. "I cannot lie under that comforter, Sorin. I'm already a little warm." Imagining myself waking up in a pool of sweat, I wrinkled my nose. He swung his legs over the edge and quickly fluttered to me at the foot of the bed. I spun around. It was still a little jarring to see him move so swiftly. He offered his hand. I took it and slipped off the bed, curious. He led me a few steps and then fluttered away again. There was a blur of satin, and the drapes on the edge of the bed stirred in response. Everything stilled before me. Sorin was back in bed, pillows propped up between him and the wall. The velvet-and-satin comforter peeked out from the black satin sheet that lay over the entire bed. He reached over and pulled the sheet back for me. I couldn't help grinning as I joined him. I lay on top of the velvet comforter and turned on my side to face him.

Sorin lifted the smooth black sheet to my shoulder. "Better?" he asked, a twinkle in his eyes.

I realized, in that moment, that the simple act of rearranging the bedding for my comfort meant so much to him. "A great improvement," I offered, laying my head down. I had not noticed it before, but my pillow lightly smelled of sandalwood. "Sorin … have you really slept in my bed the past few days?" My stomach stirred a little at the thought.

"Lain … not slept," he corrected me. "The bed smelled of you … it faded a bit more each day. However, now you are back in it." A grin teased his lips. "Mia, I could not imagine being anywhere but at your side—or, at the very least, surrounded by your scent." His eyes slowly closed, and he rested his head on the wall behind him. Taking a deep breath, his chest filled with air. "Orange blossoms … and honey," he whispered to himself.

I lay there watching him. He was so calm and content. I felt jealous. He sat straight up suddenly, his eyes opening. I jumped at the sudden movement. He looked at me apologetically and squeezed my shoulder as a sorry. I sighed and tried to relax again.

Sorin opened the nightstand drawer and lifted out his phone. It was the first time I had seen him with it and wondered if something was wrong. He pressed so many numbers, I thought it too many, but I understood as soon as he spoke.

"Allo," he said politely to the person answering on the other end. There was a pause. I could just make out a male's voice on the other end. It was quiet and responded in French. Sorin spoke again. "Puis-je parle à Monique Veuillez … Sorin." Another pause, and he smiled as he looked down at me. I scowled in confusion. I heard a woman's voice after a minute, and their conversation began. He looked forward and smiled lightly. "Allo, Monique."

I quickly wished I had remembered more of the French I had learned back in high school. I focused on his expression, the tone of his voice, and strained to hear the woman on the other end. She sounded excited, but then her voice took on a scolding tone. Sorin's expression turned to light irritation, but he still smiled slightly. I guessed that they hadn't talked in awhile and she was expressing her opinion on it. He agreed to whatever it was she had just said, but not wholeheartedly. Then he asked her something. … No it was a request. I recognized a few words. The color orange and maybe something about a few days. Then he gave my address, and I knew he was ordering something, possibly from Paris. He started thanking her but stopped.

I heard her voice. "*Ahh* … Sorin." A realization of some sort, but then her voice became sultry and she continued slowly. I started to feel unnerved until Sorin's face lost any of the amusement it had held a minute before. I listened more closely; she was speaking in a seductive voice, but there was a ring to it. I relaxed; she was teasing him. "Lourds enfin trouvé quelqu'un?" His eyes lowered to the foot of the bed, and his jaw flexed. "Oui," he finally said, as if she had forced a confession.

Monique's voice rose slightly, and she started speaking very quickly. Sorin shook his head and said no a few times. There was a pause on both ends. When she spoke again my blood heated. She sounded like she had a moment before, only no teasing this time. Her voice was pure female, feline; it purred. Sorin's body lay back against the wall, his expression blank. Monique's voice continued. "Est-elle là avec vous maintenant?"

On the last word I heard it was a question. I rose on an elbow, feeling cross, and the satin sheet slid down to my waist. Sorin finally whispered "oui" in response. She asked him another question, more slowly this time. "Prévoyez-vous d'enfin s'engager à quelqu'un?"

His eyes drifted from the foot of the bed to my feet. His head only turned half toward me, but his eyes continued. They inched their way up my body, lingering at my knees, then my hip. His face stayed blank, but my skin could feel his gaze, even through the fabric. My body relaxed, and my heart started to quicken in my chest. His eyes kept their course, pausing at my stomach and then my chest. My pulse increased even more, and I pulled the sheet to my breast, clinging to the fabric. Sorin's eyes crept higher, resting on my neck. Once his gaze touched my bare skin, it heated, tingled. There was a spot just above my collarbone that quickly warmed. His gaze moved to my lips, and I could see his eyes more clearly. They burned into my lips. I couldn't help but react by biting my lower lip. His eyes were glazed over, looking at me but taking in so much more. I bit my lip a little harder and tried to fight the pounding in my chest. Sorin's eyes finally met mine, and time stopped. My head instantly lightened. I thought the room had moved, but my body had just returned to the bed below me, and I lay on my side. His eyes continued their torture, heated and hungry.

He finally broke the silence with a simple "oui", only the single word made my head swim. His voice matched what his eyes were saying. He was in a haze but looked at me in a way I had never seen a man look at a woman. When he said yes it sounded so primal. My eyes closed as my heartbeat pounded in my head. I saw him in my mind, eyes burning into me. My body lay before him. The phone slipped from his hand and fell to the bed. Sorin reached out and grabbed a fistful of the satin sheet that lay between us. His jaw tightened, and he slowly pulled the sheet to him. It slipped through my fingers, and a whimper escaped me. He repeated the action; each time, my heart jumped, and his eyes slowly grew more focused. The sheet no longer covered me—it had become a ball of fabric on his lap. Sorin then brushed it to the floor with a final movement of his hand. I eased from my side to my back and stared at the ceiling, my arms just lying at my sides. I felt the bed shift, and Sorin leaned over me. My whole body quivered below him. I felt like a sacrifice lying before him. I was still, anticipating his next movements.

Off in the distance I heard Monique's sultry voice ask another question. "Quelle couleur serait allure sur elle?"

Sorin breathed quietly. "Quelque chose noir ou cramoisi."

The Frenchwoman laughed, and my eyes shot open.

I had imagined it all, just as I had in the kitchen. In reality I was still lying on my side, holding the sheet to my chest. I looked at Sorin, confused. The haze slowly lifted from his face, and he blinked. Monique was still rambling away excitedly, her shrill voice the only current sound in the room. Sorin removed the phone from his ear and shook his head. His face twisted in disgust as he looked down at the phone he held. In a flash he was standing at the side of the bed, berating her in French.

I had followed the conversation pretty well at first, but now it had reached a point where I suspected she was asking him about me. Suddenly Sorin was pacing and scolding Monique. Words flew so fast, I couldn't translate a single one. He paused and waited; for an apology, I assumed. I heard a quick quip on her end, and then the phone beeped as she ended the call. Sorin just looked at the phone in surprise. He opened the nightstand drawer, his phone in, and then slammed the drawer shut.

I winced at the noise of the drawer slamming and sat up, facing him. He looked down at the nightstand and mumbled what I thought were far from pleasantries in French. My head had cleared, and Sorin's seemed completely out of the trance I had seen him in moments before. It didn't know what to do or say. I wasn't clear on all that had just transpired.

I lightly coughed and whispered his name. He stopped mumbling and turned toward me, but stayed silent. I could see he didn't really want to talk about it, but I wanted some answers. Who was Monique to him? A friend? A love interest? … Didn't I have a right to ask? I felt most of their conversation had been about me. I was extremely curious about the last four questions he had answered while in a complete fog. I leaned to his side of the bed and pulled back the comforter. "Come back to bed," I urged gently.

He glanced down at my hand on the bed and forced a smile. "If you wish, Mia." His words sounded hollow.

I had to ask. "What was that all about?" I tried to keep my tone light.

He climbed back into bed, slipping under the comforter and lying on his back. I sat there and waited. The tension slowly drained from his body. Tucking his right arm under his head, he laid his left arm on top of the sheet between us. Eventually he spoke "I ordered something for you." I could hear irritation lingering in his voice.

I had gathered he was getting something for me. It was what they had said after that part that I had become desperate to understand. Looking at me, his expression begged me to let the subject go. "Thank you." I smiled weakly and then lay down. I stared at the wall, trying to decide whether to try to go to sleep or fight it a little longer.

"Go to sleep, Mia. ... We have tomorrow." His voice still held a slight plea.

The word sleep echoed in my head, and I remember his statement earlier. "Do you sleep?" I asked, wondering what his comment had meant.

"Every living thing needs rest. I just need much less than you do."

I turned my head to see his face. He stared blankly at the ceiling. "So you just lay here while the sun is up?" I asked gently. "What do you think about?" I had said it without thinking. I opened my mouth to say how sorry I was.

But before I could, he turned on his side, facing me. His face wore a light smile. "For the past twenty-four years ... every day, I thought of you. Before that, nothing of true importance." His voice was content, and I blushed lightly.

I lay on my back and moved closer to his side. He returned to resting on his back. My right arm brushed his where it lay between us. I pictured how he had touched his wrist when describing that night all those years ago. I slipped my hand under his and intertwined our fingers. Sorin's hand was cool to the touch. I lifted our hands off the bed and angled them over my chest. With my left hand I reached over and pushed his sleeve back. Not seeing anything, I moved his sleeve farther, and there they were. I would not have noticed them without knowing what to look for. His scars were just a shade lighter than the surrounding skin. I ran my fingertips over them—two slightly raised parallel lines just below the crease of his elbow.

Images quickly flooded my mind. "Sorin ... What was it like ... for my mother?" I wondered what she must have thought of the whole encounter with him. "I mean, what did she think of what you did?" I couldn't decide if I was saying it correctly. My fingers played over his scars.

"I do not completely understand your inquiry, Mia." I heard uncertainty in his voice. "I am sure there are so many details of myself and my kind that I have yet to mention or explain. Not that I am trying to keep them from you. I just think to try explaining all the differences between us at once would overwhelm you. Do not worry about your mother. She forgot all about me and what I did for her." He paused, trying to figure out how to explain it to me, I assumed.

My left arm fell to the bed, but I continued to look at his scars.

When he continued, his voice took on a very controlled, thoughtful tone. "I tore my skin and pressed my bleeding arm into her abdomen. ... Her wound quickly healed. She was so focused on you and Jennifer that she did not realize what I was doing until I finished. I did have to give her

137

a superficial wound to explain the blood on her clothes." He paused, touching his scars briefly. "The moment I saw some kind of realization, I ... I looked into her eyes and told her to forget what I had just done." He stopped and let his arm grow heavy, so I let it fall back to the bed.

Keeping my right hand under his, I rested my head against his upper arm. "You just made her forget everything you did for her—everything about you? ... You can do that?" My voice was quiet. It was getting more difficult to fight the urge to close my eyes.

"Those who are weak-minded, or who want to forget, can be persuaded mentally. Your mother did not wish to remember, so it was easy for her to forget. I reminded her that there were more important things than how she had survived. To focus on what mattered most and forget the rest." Sorin propped himself up on his elbow. Facing me, he lightly traced the frame of my face with his fingers. "I could make you forget everything, Mia—everything about me—if that were what you truly wanted."

His voice was so low and vacant. He wasn't really offering me the option, just stating aloud the possibility. The last thoughts before I drifted off were of wondering what I would choose. Could I return to being oblivious to his kind existing? I hadn't really thought about other vampires; Sorin was all I knew. Clips of vampire movies I'd seen flitted through my mind, passing behind my closed eyes. And then sleep finally came. Darkness at last. ...

Chapter 12

I awoke to Sorin gingerly squeezing my arm. "Mia … Mia, your phone is ringing." I blinked a few times. My eyes burned; it must have been only a few hours after I'd fallen asleep. I reached toward my nightstand, where I usually kept my phone, but couldn't put my hands on it. "Your phone is downstairs in the guest room," he offered.

I stopped fumbling for it. "What time is it?" I asked, turning toward him. The room was dark, and it was hard to see him.

"The sun has only been up a short time." He spoke quietly, giving me a chance to acclimate. He turned on the small lamp that sat on his side of the bed.

I slipped out from under the sheet and rubbed my eyes. I opened my bedroom just wide enough to squeeze myself through the space, wondering what the actual rules of exposure to sunlight were. I shut the door behind me and leaned against it. The sun was pouring in through the glass in the front door and surrounding windows. I had been sleeping during the day and waking up in the just before sunset for the past few days. Between my current sleeping habits and lack of sleep, the sunlight was overpowering.

I made my way to the downstairs guest room. Standing in the doorway, I heard my phone beep a voice mail notification. I stepped into the room, waiting to hear it again. I didn't see my phone on the nightstand or vanity, and I was still too disoriented to remember where I had left it. The beep sounded again, and I looked near the wall; there it lay on the floor. It came back to me. It rested where I had thrown it two nights earlier.

I sat on the floor, pressed some buttons to retrieve the message, and listened. It was the owner of a little pizzeria that was to be opening soon. He wanted to know if my services were available for some paintings. He left his phone number, saying he had seen my work in the local bank and coffee shop. I didn't bother to write down his name or number. I just shut my phone and let the message stay saved for later.

I went to the kitchen, poured a glass of orange juice, and drank it. After setting the empty glass in the sink, I returned upstairs, opening my door just enough to slip back in. I shut the door behind me and crossed to the bathroom to brush my teeth.

I put my toothbrush away just as Sorin's voice called from my bedroom, inquiring, "Who was it? ... If it is not too forward of me to ask." He sounded curious.

I walked to the side of the bed, crossing my arms. He lay buried under the covers of my bed. "Sorin ... during the past five days, you have confessed to saving my mother's life and mine. So much as said you killed the man responsible for the attack that same night. You have invited yourself into my bedroom ... my bed. But you are worried asking about a phone call is too forward." I could see trying to point out the irony was lost on him. Then I wondered why he even had to ask. "Couldn't you hear the message from up here?" The night before, when I'd spoken aloud my request for shampoo and body wash, he had heard it all the way in the kitchen and come upstairs with the items I'd asked for.

"I do not enjoy listening in on others' conversations, Mia."

I was slightly puzzled. "But you can hear me downstairs, right?" I asked.

"Yes … but I can also tune out noise if I wish to." It was a simple explanation. "So who called you?"

I walked over, shut off the lamp, and crawled back into bed. "Just a local restaurant owner wanting me to do some paintings for him. Probably grapes and wine bottles, that kind of stuff." I bunched the pillow under my head and closed my eyes, which were still irritated from being awoken so early.

The dark room was silent for a few minutes. "Are you going to accept the offer?" He spoke quietly now that the light was off.

I sighed. "I do not feel like painting. I don't feel like talking to anyone outside this house … Actually, I don't even feel like leaving this room right now." I meant it all, but I wondered how many more days I could go without facing anyone outside this house.

"Mia, you should do it. The world has not stopped out there. Though I am sure you feel as if it has." Sorin's hand ran down my arm and squeezed my hand.

I lay there, remembering being in the attic the week before. Tears started filling my eyes. "I was painting when Jennifer called to tell me about my parents' accident." My voice cracked, and I rolled over, burying my face in his chest.

Sorin wrapped an arm around me, holding me tight. Leaning over, he kissed the top of my head. "I am sorry,

Mia. ... I had no idea ... I have only just recently entered your life again. Please forgive me."

He rested his head against the top of mine as I tried to calm myself. "I cannot just perk up and start painting stupid fruit or sappy landscapes right now." I slowly relaxed further. "I'm just really tired, and I need to go back to sleep. I don't want to talk about this right now. "

I was gradually becoming upset with myself. Both for letting this bother me so much and for turning to Sorin for comfort so quickly. I turned my back to him, staring into the darkness. Any progress I had made over the past days seemed to slip away. I pulled the sheet up to my chest, wanting to make it all just go away. I wiped away the tears that filled my eyes and eventually fell back to sleep.

Sky and water lilies filled my vision. I looked around. I was on the dock with water lilies all around me. This time the lilies spread out as far as I could see, and just a few spots of water were visible. I slowly stood up and looked out; it was beautiful. The white flowers filled the water, pressed close against one another, petals touching.

I became aware I was dreaming. I knew where I was and turned to see my father. He wasn't real. All of this wasn't real. But I didn't care this time. I turned, and there he was with little Mia. Just like every time before, the childhood me leaned toward the water. As always too, my father grabbed little Mia, lightly scolding her. I wanted to go over to him this time, throw myself into his arms. Tell him how much I missed him. I stood and watched, waiting for him to pick a flower from the water.

The clouds swirled, becoming dark in seconds, and I looked up at them in confusion. Everything was different this time; something was wrong. I looked back down at my father, suddenly uneasy. He didn't notice the clouds changing above him. He reached down to pick a water lily for me. Everything slowed down around me. My father's fingers slipped under the water to cup the flower in his hand.

My heart started pounding, and I opened my mouth to warn him. Something was very wrong—my voice failed. He leaned closer, half of his body over the edge of the dock. Multiple arms reached up from the water, pulling my father in. My eyes widened in horror. I tried to run to his side, to keep him on the dock. But my legs would not move; all I could do was reach out to him. Everything returned to normal speed. My father splashed and kicked frantically as he was pulled underwater. Little Mia started screaming and backed away. The screams echoed in my head, and I covered my ears. All I could do was helplessly watch the scene before me unfold.

Eventually the water stilled, and the flowers returned to the place where he had been pulled under. I squeezed my eyes shut, shaking my head. I tried screaming again. This time my screams left my throat, raw and heartbroken, drowning out little Mia's shrill panicked ones.

Chapter 13

I opened my eyes. It took me a minute to realize I was in my room. I sat up in my bed and looked around, still half searching for my father. I was reaching out to something in front of me that wasn't there. A few candles flickered from across the room. It started to fully sink in—not just where I was but also all that happened.

I turned and reached to the other side of the bed. Sorin was gone; I was alone. My body shook, and I started crying, pulling the sheet to my face.

The bedroom door flew open, and Sorin was instantly at my side. "Mia?" His voice was full of worry. "Are you awake?" He moved closer, wrapping his arms around me.

I looked up at him and then burst into tears. "He left me!" I gasped. "He was there ... right there. ... And then gone ... just gone." My body shuddered, and I couldn't catch my breath.

"A dream, Mia. You just had a bad dream. ... And it is over now." Sorin reached up and began to dry my tears.

I jerked away from him, fought his embrace. "A dream?" I gulped between gasps of air. My eyes narrowed, and I tried to shove him away. "It wasn't a dream, Sorin. They are gone. ... My parents left me." My voice became louder, and my head started to throb.

He moved from my side and backed against the wall near the bedroom door. His eyes cast their beautiful reflection as the candlelight caught them. But they weren't their usual ice-blue with silver. They were a darker blue this time—sapphire. He glanced away from me, a mixture of emotions on his face. Finally he crossed his arms over his chest and looked back at me. "They did not leave you, Mia!" His voice matched mine, and my body stiffened. "Your parents were taken from you. … It was not their choice. It was tragic. Their lives were ended prematurely." His voice lowered, and compassion crept in. "Mia … they did not leave you." He relaxed and leaned against the wall behind him.

Without warning, all my emotions erupted, directed at Sorin. My hands tightened into fists, and I leaned toward him. "Do not tell me how I feel, Sorin! I feel abandoned … like they left me." My heart ached, and the tears started filling eyes again. "Inside I feel empty." I placed a palm over my chest. "And my heart hurts, literally … as if it's broken." I slid my hand over my heart. "It hurts so much! …" I cried, slowly shaking my head. "I can't do this, Sorin." I wiped my tears away and looked down at the bed, closing my eyes.

My mind drifted, and I saw my parents' caskets surrounded by roses. My heart physically hurt, my head throbbed, and my whole body seemed to ache. *I can't do this,* I thought. *I don't want to do this anymore.* Every time the reality of my life hit me, I wanted it to end. *No more!* I screamed in my head. I instantly decided I didn't have to continue; I could end my pain. I opened my eyes and started looking around my room.

"Mia?" Sorin's voice was quiet but filled with suspicion. I paused and looked at him. He took a step toward me, tilting his head slightly. A few wrinkles appeared on his forehead.

My color, I quickly thought. I stilled myself, as if not moving or looking around would hide my intention. I continued to consider my options, not saying a word to Sorin. I took a couple of deep breaths to calm myself. I had to focus, gather my thoughts. I tried to clear my mind, thought of blue skies and puffy white clouds. I really had no idea what Sorin saw when he looked at me or how much of my thoughts and feelings he could sense. I looked at him, into his still-sapphire eyes for a minute. Then I feared he would see right through me, so I looked away. I tried to survey the room again, slowly and calmly this time. It was pointless. He had thrown out all the pills Gina given me. There wasn't a possibility of anything sharp or deadly lying around my room.

"Mia?" His voice rose drastically, and I looked up at him. My heart fell a little; it didn't matter what I wanted. Sorin was just feet from me, and he would not let me hurt myself. My mind kept searching for an option—something … anything. "You are up to no good, Mia," he finally accused.

"I am not," I whispered, hoping to convince him. I looked at him as a realization suddenly dawned on me. Maybe trying to figure out a successful form of ending my life wasn't the correct path—at least not while Sorin was around. Hovering near, with his eyes burning into me. Maybe Sorin was the method. I did have something life-ending in my room, after all. He was a vampire. It was in his nature to kill. My mind started to scramble for a way to make it happen. Maybe if I pushed him, made him mad. Would he attack me—kill me? I was unsure.

There were still so many gaps in my knowledge of vampires. In the movies there was always violence. Vampires were violent, bloodthirsty creatures. They usually drained humans and left them for dead. But I would at least have to provoke him, push him to the edge somehow. I sat there and continued to plot. How to enrage him to the point of no self-control. I looked around the room again.

He said my name again, accusing me of something. He wasn't sure what yet. I was slowly losing hope. I didn't know him well enough to accurately choose a subject to upset him with. I thought some more. Maybe upsetting him wasn't the way, either. My eyes searched the mirror above my dresser. Recalling every little item on my dresser but deciding crossing the room was too risky. I was about to give up. Then I saw a reflection of them in the mirror.

There on the nightstand beside me were the roses Sorin had picked and brought to my room the night before. I pictured their thorns. Not words but blood would provoke him. I looked away from the dresser, trying to keep my intentions hidden. I looked at the floor and then up to Sorin's face. His eyes were so vivid in color that I could tell he was trying to figure something out. I wondered if I could trick him somehow. Maybe if I tried to think about one thing but really felt something else. Would it disguise my true intent?

I said the first thing I thought of. "Where were you? ... When I woke up you weren't here." I tried to sound either hurt or curious. I wasn't sure which came across.

He stood perfectly still, not moving a muscle. "I was outside ... getting some fresh air and making a few phone calls." Nothing changed in his eyes, and his arms stayed crossed over his chest. It wasn't working. "I did not want to wake you, so I stepped outside. I had no idea you were going to awake so abruptly, Mia." His tone was flat; he was still on alert, not trusting that I wasn't up to something.

I didn't miss the apology at the end. A part of me cringed. Even now, after I'd yelled at him and he knew that I was still scheming—"up to no good," as he'd put it. And yet, he still felt sorry for not being there for me when I woke up distraught. I was not to be deterred. I thought harder, deciding on my next topic.

I moved back to my side of the bed and sat against the wall. The simple repositioning made Sorin close the space between us. I worried I had given myself away somehow. He stood against the side of the bed, near my feet. He waited, studied me for a minute. Doubt still filled his face.

"Sorin?" I began hesitantly. "Do you have … fangs?" My eyes slowly drifted down to my hands in my lap. I tried to act nervous about asking. But I was really trying to see how close to the vase I had positioned myself. I let my eyes drift up to my elbow. I could see the mix of red and pink flowers out of the corner of my eye. I quickly looked back at him, trying to look interested in the coming answer.

"Yes," he eventually stated, his voice devoid of any emotion.

Once I had his confirmation, I actually became intrigued. I had considered the possibility but had never seen them. So I'd assumed that it was another vampire feature that books and movies had embellished over the years. He had never given me a real toothy grin, just soft smiles, usually with his lips closed.

"Smile," I said rather rudely, the sudden confirmation confusing me. He smiled, but it didn't reach his eyes; it was more like bearing his teeth for a few seconds. I tried to look closer, but his mouth returned to the tight line it had been before. I felt even more puzzled, certain I hadn't glimpsed any fangs. "You're lying," I accused, folding my arms across my chest.

He didn't move a muscle, but his expression slowly eased. "Am I?" he challenged, his tone slightly lighter than it had been in the past moments. I had momentarily forgotten what I'd already learned. If he had been lying, I should have had that bitter taste in my mouth that I'd experienced before.

My shoulders fell. No bitter taste; he was telling the truth. "So where are they?" I blurted out. "I mean … I didn't see them." I couldn't help but let a smirk come over my face. "Can I see them?" I pressed, suddenly excited at the thought.

Sorin stepped back, and his eyes circled me. "You are curious about my having fangs. … But why I wonder?" His arms relaxed.

I scrambled for something to say, something would make him lower his guard more. I tried to ease the tension in my body so I would seem flippant about it. "You know, a girl shares her bed with a vampire … and she becomes a little worried about certain details. Fangs being one of those concerns." I shrugged my shoulders and smoothed the sheet out over my lap, hoping it would work.

My heart skipped a beat as he stepped forward and sat on the edge of the bed, near my feet. Sorin finally looked somewhat at home. I wondered if it mattered how close he was when I cut myself with the thorn. It couldn't hurt to have him closer and then bleed right under his nose. I pulled my legs up and tucked them closer to myself. It worked. He moved closer, and concern seemed to come over him. "Mia, my fangs are nothing for you to be anxious about. I promise they pose no threat to your life." Sorin's voice was gentle and full of assurance.

I started to worry that this wouldn't work, after all. I began to panic inside. It must have showed. "What else?" He asked, placing a hand over mine.

In that moment, I realized he was no longer suspicious of anything. I slowly moved my hand away, so it would be free to pick a rose from the vase. A look of hurt crossed his face, but it passed. "How often?" I asked in a hushed tone. I wasn't sure how to word my inquiry. I could see he did not understand the question. I tried to make it clearer, but not too blunt. "How often do you … use your fangs?" I couldn't help but cringe a little. "For their intended purpose?" I hoped my topic of conversation would distract Sorin from what I was about to do.

"My … nutritional requirements are yet another subject you do not need to worry yourself with, Mia." He relaxed even more, waiting for my response.

I took a deep breath and slowly exhaled, trying to stay calm. I tried to picture myself nonchalantly picking up a rose. Maybe admiring it for a few minutes and then suddenly puncturing my skin with its thorn. If "my color," as he put it, showed the anxiety I was feeling he misunderstood the reason. But it seemed to be working, so I continued. I started fidgeting with the sheet over my lap. "Maybe I'm not so much worried about your fangs or eating habits as simply curious." I let my left arm drift to the edge of the bed near the nightstand.

Sorin's face held a scowl for a minute, but he finally gave in. "What do you want to know, Mia? But, understand, I do not feel this topic is an appropriate one to discuss so soon after. …" His voice trailed off.

Death was all around me; visions of vampires hunting and bloody confrontations filled my mind. I wasn't bothered by the potential of their being accurate. "I am fine … I've just been wondering ever since you told me you were a vampire, that's all." I looked down at the bed and tried to act as if I'd just noticed the roses on the table next to me. I started to reach for one and suddenly couldn't remember which variety had larger thorns. My mother had at least five diverse varieties of roses around the outside of the house. They were different colors, had different fragrances, and had thorns in a range of sizes. At the last minute, I plucked a dark-red rose over the bright-pink one next to it. I simply laid it in my lap and turned my attention back to Sorin. Thankfully, he was still distracted by my interest in his activities as a vampire. "So, how often?" I pressed. I raised the rose to my face and smelled it. My heart skipped a beat, and I had the urge to just squeeze one of the thorns into my palm.

Sorin's shoulders straightened, and I immediately forced a smile and lowered the rose. "Unless I've missed something … it's not three meals a day."

His scowl returned briefly. "No … it is not necessary to consume blood daily for my kind to survive."

He paused, and I slowly moved my fingers over the top of the rose's petals while cupping it in my other hand. He continued to explain as I half listened. Something about the quality of the blood and the amount could appease a vampire's thirst for quite a while. I looked at the rose, tilting it to examine the thorns. I let out a small sigh; I'd picked the right rose.

I focused my attention back on Sorin. "So how long has it been for you?" I raised an eyebrow and really wondered about the answer. Maybe it would affect his reaction to what I was about to do. His lips pressed together, and I could see him trying to decide whether to divulge that information. My heart started to beat faster as I considered that maybe it had been so long ago that he had to struggle to even recall it.

"It has been longer than normal for me." He spoke cautiously.

My pulse increased further, and then I slipped my fingers from the rose petals to the stem. I started to pick out a thorn to puncture my skin with.

Sorin's face changed. He reached out and cupped the right side of my face in his hand. "Mia … just because it has been an extended time since I fed last does not mean you are in any danger. I can control myself." His voice was trying to reassure me, only I was optimistic it was a lie. Or at least not completely revealing all the details; I knew I would know if it was lie.

I slipped my left hand under the rose and tilted my wrist up toward it. I leaned my face more into his hand, further distracting him. I kept a few fingers on the thorn I decided to use, lining it up with the softest parts of my other wrist. My heartbeat started pounding in my ears. Sorin released my cheek, and his hand dropped to his lap. Distrust filled his face, and I could tell he saw or sensed something.

I leaned toward him and looked deep into his eyes. "Can you really control yourself, Sorin?" I took a quick breath. "Because I'm guessing it's just instinct, like that of a shark when it smells blood." I wished it true as I pressed the thorn into my flesh. I had planned on raking the rose's thorn all the way from my wrist to my elbow. But no sooner did I feel the tip of the thorn touch my skin than Sorin knew my intention. He tore the rose from my hand, turned on the overhead light, and was beginning to pace along the wall to my right—all before the gasp finished escaping my lips.

I blinked a few times to adjust to the room in full lighting, and the stinging from my hand registered. I looked down and opened my right hand. There were a few thin red lines where the thorns had caught my skin as he tore the rose from my grasp. The cuts were minimal and caused only a faint sting.

I looked back up at Sorin, who continued to walk back and forth from my bedroom doorway to my dresser. He was oblivious to my hand and the thin lines of blood it held. Tears filled my eyes. "But ... the blood," I said to myself, defeated.

Sorin halted, turning to face me. "Enough, Mia!" His voice boomed, and I couldn't help but jump in response. His face was full of frustration and irritation. He crushed the rose in his hand and let it fall to the floor. He did not bother to refrain or spare my feelings in any way. "Is this what you really want, Mia?" His hands were clenched at his sides. "Is this what your parents would want for you?" The pacing resumed. "You are not the only one hurting, the only one in pain." Everything Sorin said caused a knot to form in my throat. "I came here days ago, and this house was full of people who absolutely loved and adored your mother and father. Jennifer feels as if she has lost a sister. ... But you have not talked to her in days. The moment your mother's life ended, a part of me was forever lost." He paused in both stepping and speaking. Sorin slowly lifted a hand to his chest and uncurled his fingers. He turned to face me, and I saw the pain and sorrow in his eyes. "I feel empty too. ... I lost a part of myself. ... I cannot bear the thought of losing you also. I understand this is overwhelming. You do not want this life anymore—so be it, Mia." His hand lowered, and he crossed the room to my side, sitting on the edge of the bed and brushing a few loose hairs from my face. "But please consider allowing me to offer you another life, if you are so set on ending this one."

I could see the desperation on his face and hear it in his voice. He couldn't imagine the thought of losing even more of himself. I just sat there staring at him, unable to speak. I tried to process the alternative he was proposing. I was increasingly experiencing moments of not wanting to live another day. And yet, here was Sorin, offering to prolong my life. Minutes passed, and my mind still raced. This had been Sorin's true reason for seeking me out at this time. He'd found me to help me through the tragedy I was experiencing. To ease what pain he could, in turn, lessening the hurt he felt within. But it was that instinct to complete the bond he'd denied himself years ago that drove him—had driven him, all along. What if it wasn't what I wanted?

He leaned forward and kissed my forehead. "I am sorry, Mia. I have only added to your stress. To suggest that you allow me to turn you. ..." He glanced away briefly. "It would not to be in your immediate future, however. You could take some time to consider my offer." His voice softly drifted off, and I wondered what he wasn't saying.

"Why not in my immediate future, Sorin?" Not that I wanted this tonight—or even at all—but I wondered, just the same.

His mouth twitched ever so slightly, and he took his time answering. "I am suffering right now, Mia. I am grieving over the loss of your mother." The desperation returned to his face. "If I were to turn you now—if we were to fully bond while you were in this pain—I honestly do not know if I could endure that. To amplify all of your emotions at the same time as the grief that I feel currently. It would be pure hell ... for me and for you. It would only be torture for both of us." His voice sounded so sad, and yet I still couldn't totally comprehend being able to physically feel each other's pain and sorrow.

I said the only thing I could. "I need some time to consider your offer, Sorin. ... I'm sure you understand what kind of decision this is." I tried to say it as gently as possible.

Sorin eventually stood up and left the room. I stayed where I was, staring after him.

Chapter 14

After a few minutes, I decided to join Sorin downstairs. I went to the bathroom to freshen up. Stepping on the scale, I discovered I had lost more weight than I thought. I sighed and made my way downstairs, not caring to change out of my nighttime attire. I glanced at the front room when I reached the bottom of the steps, but it was empty. I expected to see him in the kitchen, sitting on a stool and waiting for me. The kitchen was vacant but lit. I passed a few bananas on the counter. They had turned brown, and I tossed them into the trash. I tried to be optimistic that something in the fridge would appeal to me. Everything I picked up was near or past its expiration date. Out of frustration I pulled the trash can from the cupboard and disposed of nearly all the refrigerator's contents. And then I washed my hands and left the room, carrying a single green apple and a handful of pretzels.

I was beginning to wonder if Sorin was here at all. I walked to the downstairs guest room, just about to enter it, when I caught sight of some movement on the patio. I opened the patio door and stepped out, seeing Sorin. He had moved from the patio where he'd stood a moment before. Now he was a good thirty feet ahead of me, crossing toward the woods. I slumped into a chair, deciding Sorin wanted to be alone. Nibbling from my apple, I waited for him to disappear through the trees. He took another step or two and then sat down in the grass. I ate my handful of pretzels while I continued to watch him.

Leaning back on his elbows, he stretched his legs out in front of him. Sorin looked at the night sky. I looked up too, gazing at the stars speckling the dark blanket of sky behind them. The moon was just a bright sliver off to the side. I reflected on what Sorin had said about the stars, about people's perceptions. He looked at turning me into a vampire as a new life, a fresh beginning. I thought of it as something just the opposite—worse than death.

A few crickets chirped, and I looked straight ahead. I was no longer hungry and threw the rest of my apple into the rosebushes. Gradually loneliness crept over me, and I wanted to be next to Sorin. I was torn, not knowing if he wanted to be alone. Maybe he was still upset with me. A few more minutes passed, some more cricket chirps, and I couldn't take the silence any longer. He was just yards in front of me but not really there. I could tell even from a distance that his mind was elsewhere.

I cleared my throat, and Sorin sat up but continued to look straight ahead. "I'm sorry," I said, my voice just above a whisper. I hoped he heard me and knew I had meant it. He didn't move. I leaned forward in the chair, watching for something, any sign that he accepted my apology. My stomach started to knot up. "I don't know what else to say." My voice cracked a little, and then I saw movement. His right arm stretched out, and his hand ran over the ground beside him. I stood up and started toward Sorin, but then I stopped on the last step and sat down. What if I'd misunderstood the gesture? Maybe I wanted to join him so much that I was reading into things. I didn't want to look foolish if I was wrong. My eyes started to tear up. I felt frustrated with everything.

On top of the waves of pain and grief over my parents' deaths I was starting to feel this urge to be near Sorin. I wanted to hear his voice, inhale his scent, and feel his presence near me. I was slowly becoming needy when it came to him. This man before me whom I had known less than a week. A few tears fell down my cheek, and I wiped them away. I squeezed my eyes shut. Without thinking, I mumbled to myself, "This isn't right." I sniffed as my nose started to tingle in response to my tears.

"What vexes you, Mia?" Sorin's voice was right above me, and I only jumped slightly at his sudden presence.

I opened my eyes and looked up at him towering over me. I didn't fight the small smile I felt forming. "Vexes?" I teased. "Wow ... I don't think I have ever heard a person use that word in my whole twenty-three years of life." He offered his hand to help me up from the step. "No ... I think I heard it used in a movie once." I was gently teasing. His forehead showed a few wrinkles as he scowled, pulling me to my feet. "You do use a lot of words that—" I paused, searching for the correct words. "That most people don't use on a daily basis." I turned and headed inside.

"It will pass," he said casually.

I heard the door slide shut behind me and turned back to face him. "What to do you mean?" I asked, honestly confused.

"The vocabulary ... the accent ... it all will change, fade away." He said it with a shrug, and I leaned against the wall beside me, crossing my arms.

"What?" was all I could say in response. I felt confused and disappointed. Sorin's voice affected me so deeply; I couldn't imagine it changing. I didn't want to.

Sorin leaned against the opposite hallway wall, matching my stance by crossing his arms. "I hear so much more than you do in someone's voice, Mia," he continued to explain. "You hear obvious accents; you notice words that may not be used in this region or country. I hear all of that and so much more. My kind can pick up the slightest change in pitch. It takes very little effort for me to learn a language and even the slang used in that area." He stopped his explanation, looked down at himself, and then back at me. He pushed himself off the wall, uncrossed his arms, and lightly smiled. "We mimic with ease ... even a human's body language or hand gestures."

I realized my mouth was open in response to everything he'd just said. I pressed my lips together and went to the kitchen for glass of water. I drank it, put the glass in the sink, and then turned and leaned against the sink behind me. Sorin sat on his usual stool across the marble countertop. "So it is like an ability to adapt to your surroundings. ... So that you blend with humans?" I was never sure how to phrase my questions or concerns.

"We do not realize we do it most times." He shrugged. I smiled and shrugged back, but exaggerated the gesture. He grinned and looked amused.

I saw a thought cross his mind, a realization of something. He looked at me, doubt filling his expression. "You changed the subject," he accused, still playing it over in his mind.

"What?" I responded, trying to sound innocent but knowing I would fail.

His eyes grew larger, and his voice became a little louder. "You did intentionally change the subject. ... Just now, outside." He was surprised once he had confirmed it. "I am impressed ... and humbled. That is not an easy feat."

I gave up on denying it any further. "Yes, I managed to change the subject. It is something I have always been good at. Not as smoothly with my parents, but easily with everyone else." My voice held no remorse for what I had done.

His expression smoothed it all away. "You can tell me anything, Mia. You know that ... don't you?"

I knew it was true, as unnerving as it was. A part of me felt as if I could confide in him—tell him anything—and he wouldn't judge me. "I am feeling so unlike myself, Sorin. I am usually very in control of my emotions. I can go months without crying. I have always been very independent. Even as a child, I wanted to do everything myself. I only ask for help when I truly need it, and even then it's hard for me to do." I took a calming breath, pushing myself to press on. "My mother chose my name—Mia Zoa—it means 'my life'. I don't know why out of all the names in the world she chose this one for me. I asked her once, and she simply said she wanted a name for her daughter that stood for strength and independence. Said it in such a way. ... Like she was this weak woman who wanted more for her daughter. But my mother was never weak. She always pushed me to be self-sufficient and have confidence in myself. But she never neglected me in any way ... just gave me the freedom to learn and grow into who I am today." My eyes started to water, and I felt annoyed. I fought the tears and reluctantly resumed sharing everything I was feeling. "Only now, I feel like a completely different person. I have become a sobbing, needy basket case. I feel uncomfortable in my own skin." I looked at the floor and front of me. "I haven't had a man … in my life … who I—" Words failed me. "My last relationship was back in high school, and I never felt like I couldn't live without Gavin. Just really loved who he was and who we were together."

I looked up at Sorin, and my heart skipped a beat. He sat there staring at me, hanging on my every word. "I don't know what this is … between us. But this is overwhelming for me at times; really most of the time. I desire your presence to the point of … when you were just across the backyard I felt it was too far away from me. I am not used to wanting someone so intensely." I reemphasized what I'd already shared. My chest tightened, and I whispered, "This isn't right."

A mixture of emotions filled his face. "It is okay to want and need someone, Mia. It does not make you weak or insecure. I will stay as long as you want me." His focus turned to the fridge. "Not much left in there, I assume." He sounded drained all of a sudden. "I think it is time you go beyond your backyard or front door." There was definite concern in his voice. "You should call Jennifer tomorrow; I am sure she is worried about you. I convinced her nights ago that I would look after you and keep you safe. That you needed some space for a few days. It appears to have worked. Other than a few phone calls, she has kept her distance. However, it would be a reassuring to Jennifer if you reached out to her before

161

your undisturbed week is up." He had heard what Jennifer promised me. "You just discarded almost all of your refrigerator, Mia. ... Allow me to take you to dinner." He looked a little hopeful.

I hadn't left the house since the funeral. It had to be past midnight by now. I looked toward the wall where the clock used to hang, considering bartering dinner out for an immediate trip to the grocery store. I felt putting off any human contact for another day sounded good. I could manage the cashier at checkout, but that was about it. I nervously fidgeted as my stomach growled. "We true humans need things like food, sunlight, and social interaction." My voice was full of sarcasm. "That is what you're trying to convey ... correct?"

All the stress left his face, and a mischievous grin slowly grew in its place. My pulse quickened, and I became apprehensive. "It is the food I am most concerned about, Mia. I believe your refusal to listen to your body and sate your hunger is beginning to affect mine. As far as social interaction—" His tone turned satiny smooth, and I slowly blinked. "I am not opposed to being the only one that you socially interact with." He leaned forward on his stool, and I felt blood rush to my face. This was becoming unlike him; it was so forward. "If you wish to continue avoiding the sunlight ... Sorin means 'the sun'. And Mia. ..." His eyes slowly slid down my body and returned to my face, slightly glazed. "I could become your personal sun. Cause your skin to warm everyday if you want." He spoke in that wonderful voice that made my head light, my surroundings a blur.

A part of me felt compelled to close the gap between us. To become lost in the moment and experience what he suggested. He was looking at me in a way that was very similar to the way he had looked while on the phone with Monique. Sorin looked alert, but certainly not in total control of himself. I looked away, knowing it was my only chance of clearing my head. I took a few deep breaths and rubbed my temples.

When I eventually looked up at Sorin he was staring at the marble countertop in front of him, looking very unhappy. About his previous conduct, I assumed. "Sorin?" I said quietly. He kept his focus on the countertop, refusing to look at me. I repeated myself, stepping toward him as I said his name. He was a blur, suddenly on the opposite side of the kitchen. "What's wrong?" I asked softly.

He looked out the window, his back full of tension. "You are experiencing feelings and emotions you have not felt in years. ... And others you have never felt before. It may be hard for you to believe ... but it is the same for me." He paused. "You feel frustrated at not being able to control your emotions ... and the thought of needing someone." He stopped and shifted his position.

"Tell me, Sorin, what's frustrating you?" I hoped to coax it out of him.

"I feel that I am only complicating your life further. Possibly doing more harm than good, Mia. You did not ask for this ... for me." His voice had filled with guilt. "I feel a constant struggle within me—one I cannot begin to explain to you." His voice lowered, and his shoulders fell.

I crossed the kitchen and interweaved the fingers of my right hand with the fingers of his left. I lay my head against his upper arm. "Let me decide what I want and need."

He squeezed my hand in response. "That is just it, Mia. Every night I spend with you … every day I lay next to you—" His arm flexed against me. "The struggle to allow you to decide what you want becomes more difficult. With little effort, I could persuade you into a new life with me." He said it with disdain toward himself.

A chill crawled up my spine, and I backed away from him. I'd never felt truly afraid of him, but the thought of his forcing a decision on me—prolonging my life, being forever connected to him through a bond I was incapable of comprehending the depths of—it was too much. It was a decision I was nowhere near ready to make, and anxiety spread through me.

I stepped away from him, protectively crossing my arms over my upper body. My voice shook. "You would do that … decide my future for me?" I shook my head slowly in disbelief.

He turned to face me, pure anguish in his eyes. "I feel I chose your path for you years ago." His voice was a rough whisper.

With that, he turned and walked away.

Chapter 15

I just stood there, frozen and unable to move. My mind screamed for me to stay where I was, but every other part of me ached to follow him. The look in his eyes tore at my heart, and the tone of his voice kept replaying in my head. Sorin did not want to turn me against my will. Yet the desire seemed almost beyond his control. He told me it wouldn't be in my immediate future. That had given me a sense of peace. It was possible, if not likely, our concepts of time were drastically off. The urge to follow him only grew. I walked slowly to the steps and stopped. I could feel him watching me. I turned to the front room: still dark. Sorin's eyes caught the smallest reflection of light from the kitchen. A beautiful icy periwinkle looked back at me. I wondered if a part of him knew I wouldn't have been comfortable lying next to him right now. I lit a candle on the mantel.

He stood, arms crossed tightly, face still full of emotions. I curled up in the corner of the sofa farthest from him, pulling the blanket over myself. Sorin looked down at the blanket and then at me. We both knew it wasn't being used to keep me warm. I wondered if he could put my mind at ease. Maybe help me understand what he was feeling. "Sorin, talk to me … help me understand."

He continued to stand, looking at some unimportant place on the wall. "It is hard for me to explain it to you, Mia. The desire to be near you … was something I resisted for years. I had to go to the other side of the world to feel the pull toward you lessen. All the time feeling a part of me was void." I just sat and listened, afraid if I made a sound he would desist. "Thankfully, year after year passed and ... it became bearable. But when your ... Gavin was so abruptly taken from you, it took everything I had to stay away and not seek you out."

I looked down, remembering random moments with Gavin and then the moment when I'd placed flowers on his gravestone. The thoughts of him were bittersweet. Now that years had passed, I realized a part of me still loved him, but it was young love that held no real future. Maybe it always had been, and I'd been deceiving myself by thinking I would have spent the rest of my life with him. The truth was, I really didn't know for sure. The love was real; the future, tenuous at best. The future always is. I had loved Gavin's companionship, friendship, and acceptance of who I was. I had missed that these past years, but not beyond what I could endure.

I looked up at Sorin, but he had moved to the corner of the room where the light hardly touched him. I relaxed a little, stretched my legs, and let the blanket simply cover my lap. I propped an elbow on the back of the sofa and rested my head against my hand. I almost asked why this past week had led to a different outcome. But I knew the answer instantly. The pain I'd felt this past week was far beyond anything I felt when I lost Gavin. I was confident it was much different for Sorin this time also. Years ago, it was only my pain he'd felt. This time, he felt his own pain for the loss of my mother, as he'd told me. "And now that you are here with me?" I asked at last, wondering again about the constant struggle inside him.

I could hardly make out his form, but his eyes lifted from the floor and rested on me. "It would be so different if you could feel ... farther than this pain you keep yourself enclosed in." He spoke softly, cautiously. But Sorin's words still stung. He quickly continued. "I know that the hurt you are feeling is unnecessary." His voice turned to silk, beautiful and smooth. "I could lessen your pain." My body eased farther into the cushions, and I gently rested my head on my arm. "I can help you through this, Mia ... offer you a new life." I closed my eyes, and his voice continued to caress my skin. "A new beginning could be yours, if you want it. I understand this is. ..." Sorin paused. When he resumed speaking, his voice abruptly changed. "If you could only feel what I do." It was an alluring plea. "For decades, I have felt incomplete without you." My chest tightened at the sincerity I could so clearly hear. "Every part of me wants to be near you, wants to protect you. Offer you everything I am and all you could ever want. There is not a request I would deny you." I opened my eyes. A shade of silver and violet greeted me. "Trust me, Mia ... let me in. Tomorrow is a new day. Let us face it together, side by side. Allow me to be there for you whenever you need me. We will greet morning and not worry about the night that follows."

It sounded so easy—one day at a time. Maybe it was the best approach. "One day at a time?" I finally said aloud. Sorin slowly walked to my side and held out his hand. I knew it represented more than a simple gesture of assistance. It was an agreement. To accept a future, one that currently included him. Without a second thought, I draped my legs over the side of the sofa and took his hand. In that moment, I think we both felt a glimmer of hope. I thought of it as a step to reclaiming my life. I felt like Sorin interpreted it as a possible future with me in it. I kept my hand in his, even after I stood and led him upstairs.

Once back in my room, Sorin decided to take a shower. When he pulled his black suitcase out from under my bed, I mumbled. "You don't have to hide it under my bed anymore." He softly smiled. "The dresser in the guest room is empty," I offered. His small smile faded, and I instantly knew he had misunderstood. He closed his luggage quickly and started for the door, reaching out and taking a pillow from my side of the bed as he passed it. I moved from the bed, intending on stopping him in the doorway. But he had already entered the guest room by the time I crossed into the hallway. He must have increased his pace once he left my room.

I walked into the guest room, feeling bad as soon as I saw his face. He thought I was asking him to leave my room. I made my way to his side and sat on the bed next to his suitcase. "You are not banished," I teased. "Just your belongings. ...I have never shared my personal space with anyone like this before. It is going to take some getting used to." His face lit up once I corrected the misunderstanding. "Just keep your things in here and use this shower." He took a small pile of clothes and headed to the bathroom.

I went back to my room and waited for him to return. It was still hours before sunrise, and I thought of questions I had yet to ask him. I looked at the heavy fabric over my windows and decided to cover all the windows in the house. That way, Sorin could walk freely, despite time of day.

I was daydreaming of colors and textures to cover the windows with to block out the sunlight when he quickly entered the room. He lit all the candles. When the bedroom light shut off and changed to candlelight I pulled the comforter back for him. Sorin joined me in bed, tucking his hands behind his head.

I rolled to my right side and curled against him. "You're so warm." I blurted out. I instantly felt silly at the obvious observation. "I mean you are never cold, just cool. But right now you feel really warm." I felt a little better after explaining.

"You put anything in hot water and it warms," he teased.

I rested my left arm on his chest and started to inquire about the rules of sunlight. "Do you have to stay totally out of the sun?" I asked. "What happens if you do go out in the sunlight?" I was really just wondering out loud.

He untucked his left arm and delicately touched my bare arm that lay across him. "Do you want a detailed explanation or the shortened version?" His voice was light, warning me it was complicated, maybe even gory.

"I want to know everything … you are offering your lifestyle as an option for my future." I felt like I should learn everything I could about vampirism. So he explained in detail all there was to know. As he spoke his fingers caressed my arm, hand, and fingertips. Every word he said intrigued me. As long as vampires stayed out of direct sunlight they aged extremely slowly. Something about the body's reaction to the sun. I thought it sounded similar to photosynthesis. His fingertips studied the lines of my palm, and it relaxed me further. I continued to listen to his voice, low and smooth. I remembered the first day I met him and was sure it was early evening when I passed out. It had rained that day, with minimal sun throughout the daylight hours. "But on very cloudy days?" I asked, checking my reasoning.

"We can walk in the sun anytime we choose." Sorin's tone clearly insinuated it wasn't without cost.

"But?" I pressed.

He hesitated, and I took his hand, resting it against my cheek. He explained further, but his skin touching mine just made the words seem far away. Avoiding the sun all together was best. The stronger the sun, the more drastically vampires' blood reacted. They would age drastically as their bodies made up for the exposure they had been deprived of, and it was painful. For a young vampire, pure agony and a loss of years was the worst that could happen. For a vampire who had been a part of this world for more than a normal lifetime, it would possibly mean death possibly. Sorin reached up and released the drape near his head, and I did the same on my side. We lay for a while and watched the roses dance on the ceiling.

"So ... dinner tomorrow night ... Italian?" His voice sought approval on choice of cuisine.

"I grew up on Italian." I lightly smiled and then added flatly, "It better be authentic."

"I know an old Italian restaurant not too far from here," Sorin said.

He rolled onto his side, wrapping his arms around me and gathering my body to his. He did this with an ease that made me feel like he had taken me in his arms a thousand times before. I felt my face warm, but once I accepted his forward gesture, I relaxed. I closed my eyes and allowed my body to mold to his. I lay wondering what the next day would bring. Sorin moved me closer to him, in a full spooning position. It felt wonderful lying next to him, even if there was a comforter between us. He kissed the back of my head. "What are you thinking of, Mia?"

It was becoming increasingly effortless to answer anything he asked. "Just wondering what the future will bring." I paused. "Actually, I'm feeling a little nervous about dinner tomorrow night."

Sorin gave me a light squeeze and asked, "What are you nervous about?"

I thought about it for a minute. "I haven't left the house in several days now, Sorin. Haven't talked to anyone face-to-face other than you. A part of me wants to just continue this way for a while longer." It was saddening to say, but true.

I eventually fell asleep. No dreams greeted me.

For the second time, Sorin was waking me prematurely. "Mia, a delivery truck is outside. ...Wake up." As he said it, the doorbell rang. I blinked a few times and pulled the sheet away from me. I stood and started to stumble to the door. "Mia, just sign for the package and bring it upstairs."

I stopped and looked at him "Package?" I asked, confused.

The doorbell chimed again, and Sorin lightly smiled. "Mia, answer the door ... sign for the package ... bring it upstairs so that I can watch you open it." He motioned me to the door. I realized it was the order he had placed from Monique.

I opened my bedroom door just wide enough to walk through, stepped into the hallway, and hurried down the stairs. I cracked the front door, causing the sunlight to spill in. I shielded my eyes while accepting the clipboard handed to me. I signed it, and the woman handed me two boxes. We exchanged thank yous, and I closed the door.

Yawning, I started back up the steps. I stopped halfway and sat down in the middle of the staircase. Sorin had assumed there would only be one box. I set both boxes on the step beside me and took a closer look at them. Both were medium in size and had "fragile" stamped all over them. I lifted the first box; it felt so light, almost empty. I shook it and could hear a light crinkle, like tissue paper. I switched boxes. The second was much heavier, but no movement or sound when I tilted it.

Sorin cleared his throat loudly, and I jumped. "I'm coming!" I called up the stairs, embarrassed that he'd caught me trying to guess what the gifts were. I scooped up the boxes and returned to my room. I slipped back inside, closing the door behind me. I climbed onto the foot of the bed, next to Sorin. "Can I open them?" I asked, placing the light one on my lap first.

He scowled and sat up, his eyes examining both boxes critically. "Let me see the packages, Mia." He leaned forward and stretched out a hand. I refused to just hand them over. I could tell he was displeased about something.

"You ordered them for me … didn't you?" I held the box close to myself.

His eyes drifted from the box in my hands to the box on the bed next to me. Eventually his eyes locked onto mine, and he spoke in the voice that made the world melt away. "Please hand me the packages ... just for a minute." His voice was low and invading.

As usual my head lightened, and my surroundings became fuzzy. I couldn't refuse anything he asked of me when his voice touched me like this. I kept the light box on my lap and pushed the heavier one to his side. He picked it up, looking at it intently and tilting it sideways. I watched him listen closely and saw his nostrils flair. His face relaxed, and he passed the package back to me. He held his hand out for the box I protectively held. "Trade me." His voice flowed. I reluctantly handed over the box, and as soon as I did, irritation came over Sorin's face. He didn't smell the second package. I assumed he knew what it was simply from the weight. He brushed the comforter aside and walked from the bed to my closet.

"What are you doing?" I demanded, upset. He ignored me, putting the box on a shelf and shutting the door. "Sorin?" I said a little louder. He sat back on the bed and looked at me. "I did not ... request the contents of that box for you." I could hear him choosing his words carefully.

I sat for a minute, trying to decode everything. "So you know what is in that box?" I asked, pointing to the closet.

His lips pressed together, not wanting to answer. "Yes," he forced out.

Silence filled the air for a minute, and a hint of bitterness registered in my mouth. "How could you know what is in a closed box ... that you say you did not order?

Explain the bitter taste." I thought I should make it clear I wasn't going to lose interest so easily. "I do not know exactly what is in the package I put on your shelf. … But I know Monique, and I can guess what she sent. Monique loves to live vicariously through others. She is an amazingly talented woman … and the oldest vampire I know personally. But she injects herself into others' lives any chance she gets." His tone was irritated, and I could see he was a little uncomfortable.

I recalled how he looked while talking to her. "Is Monique … a love interest?" I couldn't help but wonder.

His face twisted, appalled at the thought. "Certainly not." he said. "An old friend that has a habit of overstepping."

Happy with the answer, I returned to the gift in question. "Is it something for me? … I mean, are the contents intended for me?" The box had felt almost empty, and his willingness to just say what it was only fueled my curiosity.

His face transitioned from irritated to simply defeated as he rested his head against the wall behind him. "Mia … the item, or items, in that box would be for you, yes. But I did not request any of it, nor do I feel it should have been sent to you without my approval. Please trust me. Promise me you will not open the box." I wasn't sure if it was in response to my expression, but after a moment, he added, "I am not saying you can never open it … just not right now."

His voice was firm, but it was obvious that whatever was in the box would upset me. Or somehow put more stress on Sorin's and my relationship. I knew I couldn't possibly persuade him to change his mind. He was only thinking of me and protecting me somehow. I looked to the closet, wondering what would upset me so much. Or maybe whatever it was would scare me, douse any hope Sorin had of my turning my back on my current life.

"Mia, just open the other package, please." He sounded disappointed. I quickly forced a smile and reached for the box, not wanting to hurt his feelings. I ran my thumbnail through the tape and carefully opened the box. I slowly moved the layer of tissue paper from the top and then edges. Carefully I opened the first ball of bubble wrap and held a beautiful crystal jar in my hand. "Open it," Sorin chuckled. The container alone was so beautiful, with intricate etchings. I didn't focus on the contents, which looked like crystals or salts. I removed the lid and pure orange scent flowed out. I inhaled deeply and closed my eyes. It wasn't diluted by vanilla or any other under note.

I opened my eyes and offered a real smile. "This is unbelievable." I closed the jar and placed it on the bed. I opened the next ball of bubble wrap. This one had a narrow body and a delicate blown-glass stopper dipped into what looked like oil inside the bottle. I put a drop on my wrist and smelled it; my smile deepened. "Orange blossoms and honey." I sighed.

"Last one?" Sorin said nodding to the box. I unwrapped the third item, another bottle with scented oil in it. I opened it and inhaled, expecting another citrus scent. But it was strong and floral, quite unexpected. I quickly lowered the bottle and rubbed my nose. I looked up at Sorin and tried to explain. "I-I thought it would be another … citrus scent," I stammered. "I like it … really. I just wasn't expecting. …" I took another sniff. "Honeysuckle?" I asked, not sure if I was correct.

Sorin's eyes narrowed as he peered at the bottle. His nostrils twitched, and he shook his head "No ... not honeysuckle. I would presume it is from a flower Monique created." His tone was serious.

"I figured she was a perfumer, not a botanist." I was pretty impressed.

"Both, actually ... Monique gets bored every three or four decades, and so she develops new interests. Not only in her professional life but private also."

I was fully impressed until I caught the possibility of his age. I discarded all the bubble wrap and placed just the bottles of oil inside the box, keeping the jar on the bed. "So how many ... professions have you known Monique for?" I asked apprehensively.

His eyes studied me, circled my body. I instantly knew what he was doing. "Does age influence your opinion of me?" His eyes circled me again. I thought about it, wondering how many centuries he had really lived. I decided not to dwell on how old he might or might not be.

I raised an eyebrow and challenged him. "You tell me."

Sorin titled his head a little and finally smiled after a minute. "It could be wishful thinking ... but no."

I crossed to my dresser and set the box down. I determined that if Sorin was going to make me leave the house tonight, I might as well run a few errands before dinner. I pulled some clothes out of my dresser.

"Mia, what are you doing?" Sorin asked, morose.

I held my clothes and the crystal jar of salts. "I am going to enjoy my gift, and then run a few errands."

The end of my explanation saddened him, and my stomach felt a few butterflies. "How long do you think you will be gone?" he asked. His eyes caught the candlelight just right, taking on that beautiful silver-blue cast. It caught me offguard; he sounded like he was going to miss me as I ran a few simple errands. It was one of the recurring moments that reminded me how complicated the past week had been.

I turned to the bathroom, and over my shoulder quietly said, "Not long." I filled the tub with water and sprinkled just a few of the crystal-like salts into the water. Pure orange scent filled the bathroom, and I started to undress. After I removed my shirt I realized the door was still ajar. I covered myself and stepped toward the door. I lightly moved it to a few-inch gap. Backing away from the door, I returned to the rug in front of the tub. I resumed undressing slowly, focusing on the bathroom door. I knew I had been far enough away from the doorway that Sorin had not seen me. When I closed the bathroom door I could only see to the foot of the bed. But the fact that I undressed without a passing thought to Sorin being only yards away distressed me. Maybe subconsciously I knew he would keep his distance. Maybe a part of me wanted to be seen by him. I slipped into the tub, feeling a touch of frustration over it all.

Candlelight spilled in from the bedroom because the bathroom door was slightly open. I lay my head back and closed my eyes, trying to relax. The citrus fragrance filled the air, and I realized I had yet to thank Sorin. "Thank you … I love the gifts," I whispered, knowing he would hear me fine.

"I am pleased you like them." His voice just reached the doorway from the bed.

My eyes burned from lack of sleep and I took a few minutes to plan my day. I wanted to find some heavy drapes, pick up fresh groceries, and maybe stop by the coffee shop to see the mama bears, show them I was surviving. The final stop would be determined at the last minute. I thought about what I could wear later that night, taking a mental inventory of the clothes in my closet. I remembered a deep-wine-colored dress with spaghetti straps. I had not worn it since Christmas, and I worried it might be a little loose. My hand slid under the water, and I rested it on my stomach. I felt mildly disgusted with myself as I continued slowly feeling different parts of my body, using both hands. My ribs felt far more predominant than usual. My hips had fewer curves to them. This wasn't my body, and I let out a sound of utter disgust with myself. I stood up, triggering the drain with my foot before stepping out. I dried off and dressed in a hurry. I flung the bathroom door open and crossed to my closet for a pair of sandals.

Sorin quickly sat up in bed. "What is wrong?" Concern laced his words. I didn't bother to look at him. I shoved my feet into my sandals and started for the door. The usual blur happened before my eyes, and suddenly Sorin stood before the door, blocking my exit. "Something is troubling you, Mia ... please tell me what it is." His fingers gently lifted my face to meet his.

I sighed. A white lie was pointless. "I am having body-image issues. I'm not the first woman to be unhappy with her body, and I won't be the last. It's not the end of the world." I said it with great exasperation. "I'm fine, Sorin, really." I brushed his hand away. "I just need to force myself to start eating better." I put my hands on my hips and nodded to the bed. He reluctantly moved aside, and I stepped out of the room.

I went downstairs, emptied the kitchen trash can from the night before, and then dragged it to the refrigerator. It was going to be a new day, a fresh start—as much as I could make it one. I opened the door and threw away the little bit left in the fridge. Every last condiment and even the box of baking soda were discarded. I then did the same to the freezer. Everything had most likely been purchased by mother and touched by my parents. I sprayed and washed it out, then took out a second bag of trash.

I returned to the kitchen briefly for my purse and sunglasses, and then I headed out.

Chapter 16

I took my time at the department store, trying to find the thickest, darkest curtains to serve their purpose. The grocery store proved a more difficult chore, as nothing appeared appetizing. In the end, I left with only a few bags, containing fruit, vegetables, milk, and some bread and pastries from the bakery. By then, it was later than expected, and I put off going to the coffee shop. Once home, I put the groceries in the fridge, along with a new box of baking soda. I nibbled on a croissant, ate a banana, and forced myself to drink a whole glass of milk. I dragged a step stool from the laundry room and then realized Sorin must be hearing all the commotion from upstairs. I considered going to him, but the thought of crawling back into bed for a few hours of sleep was too tempting.

One by a one, I took down whatever delicate sheer curtain hung on each window and replaced it with that day's purchase. By the time I was struggling with the last window on the first floor, it was approaching early evening. Each time, I tried to cover the window completely, even nailing the edges of the curtains to the wooden frame around it. Most of the windows had only a small amount of light visible from the top of the window frame. I stood in the foyer and inspected my efforts of the day, wondering if the new curtains would be sufficient. I rested my hands on my hips and yawned. I looked to my left, then to my right, eyeing each window critically. Realizing which windows would get direct sunlight, I concentrated on what to do about it. Fatigue started to set in, dulling my focus. I had done more physical activity in one day than I had in the past week.

Closing my eyes, I pictured Sorin upstairs in my bed. I thought I was imagining it at first. His hands, unhurried, slid through my arms and gently squeezed just above my hips. Without thinking a soft moan escaped my lips, and I leaned back against his body behind me. My arms lost their tension and fell at my sides. He felt so good against me. I sighed. "You have been busy." His voice was silken. "*Mmm …*" was all I could manage. "Did you do this for me, Mia?" His voice caressed my skin. My knees suddenly felt weak, and I nodded my answer. His hands lowered to my hips, squeezing them. Immediately my knees gave out below me, and I felt myself start to slip away from Sorin's body. I felt dizzy and wonderfully relaxed. I heard the chuckle as he scooped me up in his arms.

"To bed with you, Mia," he affectionately ordered. I turned in his arms, feeling the force of his body sweep us both up the stairs. I thought of the curtains and intended on asking if they were blocking out enough sunlight. But all that came out was, "Good?" My voice sounded so feeble.

Another chuckle escaped him, and he kissed my temple. "Very good," he whispered. We passed through my doorway. Sorin left the door open, carefully placing me on my side of bed and lifting the sheet over my body. I gave in to the need for a few hours of sleep, happily sinking into my bed. My pockets were full of miscellaneous items from the day's shopping that I should have returned to my purse. I gave a light whine and lowered my hand under the sheet to undo my jeans. But my fingers wouldn't obey, and I was slowly drifting farther into darkness.

Sorin's hand followed mine and gently undid the snap and lowered the zipper. He brought my hand out from under the sheet and laid it on top. I felt him at the foot of the bed, uncovering my feet. Sorin removed my sandals and let them fall to the floor. He tugged at the bottom of my jeans, and I lifted my hips briefly so my pants would lower without much effort. My eyes fluttered open, and he was neatly folding my jeans and laying them on the corner of my dresser. I rolled to the middle of the bed and waited for him to join me. He pulled the comforter over himself and moved to my side. I placed my arm over him and drifted into a deep sleep.

In my dream, I walked along the beach at midday. I could smell the salt air and feel the sun against my skin. The waves were lapping at my feet when I heard Sorin say my name. I opened my eyes and blinked a few times. Staring at the ceiling, I asked, "How determined are you about taking me out to dinner?" Lying in bed was still the most comfortable place for me.

"One day at a time," he reminded me.

I sat up in bed and turned toward him. "I left the house today, didn't I? ... Bought groceries and spoke to someone other than you."

His eyes brightened as I finished. "You visited Jennifer?" he asked, hopeful.

I looked over his shoulder. "I was referring to the cashiers at the stores." I frowned, knowing what he thought of my not reaching out to Jennifer.

He flung back the comforter, got out of bed, and went to the doorway. He turned back and shot me and a not-so-pleasant look. "I expect you ready for dinner in one hour, Mia." With that, he turned on the bedroom light and headed down the hall to the guest room.

I fell to the pillow below me, closed my eyes, and heard Sorin say my name in an annoyed tone. "Fine!" I yelled and shot out of bed, forgetting that he had removed my jeans earlier. I looked to the door, but he wasn't there. I didn't feel overly self-conscious about being half naked in my own bedroom. I blew out all the candles on the walls. Leaving my door open, I went to my closet.

I moved each article of clothing from one side of the closet to the other, trying to find what I had picked to wear. I had never realized it before, but all my clothes were dark. Sorin had pointed it out days before, but now that I looked at them myself, there was even less color than I had thought. I stepped back and looked at my closet's contents. Lots of black and grays hung before me. The clothes that were colors were all dark shades--deep plum, rich dark green, deep peacock, and burgundy. I shrugged, finally finding the wine-colored dress, taking it out, and laying it out on the bed. I reached onto a high shelf for the shoes I wanted. The box that had accompanied my gift from overseas was still sitting next to them. I brought the shoes from the shelf and set them on the floor next to the bed. I stood at the foot of the bed and peered into my closet, staring at the package just sitting there. A part of me was dying to open it to satisfy my curiosity. But I fought the urge, turned away, and dressed.

I took my time getting ready. I pulled my hair back into a loose bun, letting a few curls hang free. I applied a smoky shadow and pale lip color. I looked into the mirror when I was finished and sighed, unhappy. My cheeks had absolutely no color, which had never been an issue before, so I didn't own blush. I considered rubbing a little lipstick into them but abandoned that idea, reaching up and giving them a few good pinches instead. Sorin called my name from downstairs. I slapped the bathroom light switch and wiggled my heels onto my feet.

He stood in the foyer waiting for me, one hand behind his back. He wore a charcoal lightweight sweater and black slacks. My heart skipped a few beats as Sorin watched me descend the steps. His eyes started at my feet and slowly moved up. I felt the blood rush to my cheeks and was glad I had only pinched them. I stopped a few feet in front of him and spun slowly, enjoying his eyes on me. As I faced him again, he was holding a single short rose for me. I smiled and took it from him. Looking at it more closely, I saw the thorns had been removed. I raised an eyebrow at him. He smiled and removed the rose from my hand. "No thorns for you," he said, tucking the flower behind my ear. His fingers left the rose, traced my face, and then slid from my chin. The simple act of affection made my thoughts scramble.

I laughed nervously. "Are you trying to court me, Sorin?" I'd used that terminology because it was something I would expect from him.

He closed the small space between us and placed my open palm against his chest. He leaned in close, and a shiver climbed my spine as his lips brushed my earlobe. "Mia ... we are past the need of courting." My heart started to race at the insinuation I was already his. He lightly kissed my cheek as I moved away. He kept my hand in his, opened the front door for me, and we stepped outside.

Once at his SUV, I paused and took a step back. I hadn't noticed his windows earlier today as I passed it in the driveway. They were more than tinted; they were black. "These cannot be even close to legal," I said is as I touched them. He stepped to my side and opened the door for me, every inch the gentleman. I slid inside and settled myself in the seat.

"I could influence any law enforcement of yours to let me go with a simple warning," he remarked.

We drove for better than a half hour to the city. Talking about the curtains, he said they would block the necessary sunlight for him. He complimented my dress, and I mentioned noticing the color scheme of my clothes. I was surprised to hear that some of my tastes or interests were very similar to his. My preference for dark colors, my love of art, my never feeling overly social. All were probably not coincidences. He explained that some of my personality traits could be because of him. Sorin's voice grew bleak, and he apologized for not completely knowing the complications he might have caused my mother and me all those years ago. He finally pulled to the side of the street and parked.

I knew if I did not exit quickly, Sorin would get the door for me again. So I opened the door myself, swinging my legs out. He was at my side, looking disappointed. He held his hand out for me, and I took it, exiting the rest of the way. "Sorin, it is sweet of you, really … but you do not need to open every door for me or always lead." I tried to say it without bruising his ego.

He gave me a half smile and nodded. "I will try to remember that in the future, Mia." He shut the door, and I could instantly smell food in the air. A huge brick building took up most of the block. It looked like an old factory or a large school building; it only had a few windows.

My stomach growled before I knew it and my hand flew to it out of habit. Sorin chuckled, and I bit my lip. "Sorry … I guess my appetite is returning," I half apologized.

He started down the sidewalk and paused when I didn't follow. "What is it, Mia?" His forehead showed a few wrinkles of puzzlement.

"We're going to dinner," I blurted out. "I mean, we're going to a restaurant with food." He didn't understand what I was trying to spit out, understandably. I stepped to him and whispered, "What I am asking is, will I be the only one eating?" I assumed he didn't eat real food. He had said the mere smell of it was abrasive at times. "You said the smell of food. …"

He offered his arm to me, and I slipped my fingers into the inside of his elbow. We walked leisurely as Sorin explained. "Yes, the smell of food can be unpleasant at times, but if it means your eating a whole meal tonight … I will gladly watch and endure. But I can eat food." He waited as surprise and confusion filled my face. He smiled. "Only it would sit in my stomach for a very long time." I squeezed his arm as hard as I could. He chuckled, showing no signs of discomfort. "Our digestive systems are extremely slow. We can eat, but it is very uncomfortable having food just lie in your stomach. Plus we can taste every little thing. We get so much more nutritional value from blood."

The aroma of tomato, cheese, and bread caught my attention. My stomach announced its impatience. "It smells so good, Sorin. ... I'm starving all the sudden." I let go of his arm and walked a little faster. The sidewalk was empty, and I hurried along the brick building to my right. The streetlight on the corner ahead showed some movement. I assumed the entrance was just around the side. I was only a few steps ahead of Sorin, and I turned back to him, about to announce that I could hear music.

But the words never left my mouth. Instead, a blur caught my eye, and I froze.

Chapter 17

It all happened so fast. Sorin turned toward what had caught my attention in the streetlight just as it was upon him. He slammed against the brick wall with a horrible thud, and I jumped.

She was absolutely stunning and had her arms wrapped around him. She was petite, two to three inches shorter than I, and rail thin. Blonde wavy hair with a touch of honey color to it ended at the bottom of her back. My eyes drifted over her. She wore a mixture of fabrics in shades of gray on her upper body, and snug dark jeans hugged her thighs. Black boots laddered with silver buckles ended at her knees in a thin trim of gray fur. Like Sorin, she was overdressed for the night's temperature. The two of them were in between overhead streetlights, so I couldn't make out all the details of this new stranger.

Sorin's expression, however, was beyond surprise; he was in a state of shock. I stood frozen, not knowing what to do or say. Finally, after what seemed like forever to me, he reached up and unlocked the blonde's fingers from behind his neck. "Anya?" Sorin said in disbelief.

The girl squealed and then proceeded to gush in French, much to my dismay. *Can't anyone speak English?* I fumed to myself. Anya tried to wrap her arms around him again, but he held her at bay. She said his name, and I heard her say, "Amour."

I continued to stand motionless, and neither one of them acknowledged me. They were in their own world, oblivious to my presence only a little more than a yard away.

They went back and forth in conversation. Anya gushed about something in French, but, like Sorin, she had an accent from somewhere other than France.

Sorin's expression slowly turned to pure frustration, and he pushed her away from him. He kept repeating a single question, which she ignored: "Comment est-ce que vous trouver me?" Finally, he pushed her away.

Anya abruptly stopped fawning over Sorin, and she lifted her chin a little higher at him. Her head twitched in an odd way. She smelled the air, or maybe him; I wasn't sure which. But whichever it was caused her to turn in my direction, and a strange hiss left her mouth. I stumbled back a few steps. She spoke to Sorin as her dark-brown eyes locked on mine. Now that she faced me, I saw her features more clearly. She appeared no older than eighteen. But I knew it was just an impression. Her face showed she was absolutely repulsed by something. Her voice slowed and filled with malice. I wanted to look at Sorin for some reassurance—to know everything was all right, that I was overreacting to the sudden scene. But her eyes held mine, and I couldn't look away.

Sorin's voice boomed a short sentence in response to what she was saying. "Quitter son seul, Anya!" He filled the space between Anya and me in an instant.

She blinked a few times and raised her eyes to Sorin's. He half shielded me from her sight now. Her face took on a completely innocent look, and her body swayed gently. Her head tilted to her left, trying to see me better. "And if she wasn't here?" Anya said in a beautiful soft voice. Her sudden change in mood made me even more uncomfortable, as it was clearly fake. Her eyes slid down my body critically, as if she were sizing up the competition.

Sorin put an arm around me, pulling me toward him and further shielding me from her view. They exchanged a few more words in French. The tension grew, and my heart started to race. Sorin turned to me and cupped my face. "Do not fret, Mia … Anya is only trying to scare you. She is harmless; I swear." His voice was low and gentle. He was trying to calm me, but to no avail. I felt my heart pounding in my chest.

A slow movement caught my attention, and I looked away from Sorin. Anya had slowly circled and now was near the edge of the sidewalk. Sorin no longer stood between her and me. She took another step, still circling. Trying to find a way past Sorin. He was still talking to her, but his words fell on deaf ears. Another slow step, and Anya had moved into the edge of the overhead light. Her eyes simultaneously took on a deep-red metallic hue. She slowly smiled, and I could see a set of pearly fangs glisten. I gasped and backed up until I bumped into the brick building behind me. My blood ran cold, and the hairs on the back of my neck stood up.

"Mia?" Sorin said, concerned.

My eyes flew to his, which were currently studying the air around me. Then I looked at Anya, afraid to take my eyes off of her. She studied the air around me also, a look of pride growing. Whatever color fear was, I knew I was presently drowning in it.

Sorin turned toward Anya, and the French began again. His hands were clenched at his sides, and he stepped toward her.

But Anya had completely lost her twisted expression by the time Sorin faced her. She clasped her hands lightly in front of herself and swayed childishly. Shrugging her shoulders and batting her eyes innocently at him, she purred a response to his demanding voice. "Il n'est pas trop tard pour choisir me, Sorin."

There was a moment of utter silence, and then Sorin closed the distance between them. He delicately lifted her face to his as he stood, towering over her. She smiled brightly, free of the intimidating fangs she had possessed a minute before when she glared at me. She looked at him with absolute adoration, clearly enjoying his touch.

My heart fell as my confusion grew. I didn't know who she was to Sorin. He had told me Monique wasn't a love interest, but what about Anya? He had never mentioned her at all. The tone of their conversation and their body language made it seem one-sided—on Anya's part. But I still feared I had misunderstood it all. He kept touching her and then he lowered his face to hers, as if he were going to kiss her. I was horrified by the sight before me. My hand rested on my chest, and I felt my eyes water.

"Anya," Sorin said, his voice overly sweet.

"Oui." She sighed contently.

"Je ne sera jamais choisir vous." His voice turned hard and determined.

She stepped back, and hatred filled her face. Her eyes shot to me and then back to Sorin. She whispered a threat through gritted teeth.

Sorin's hand caught her arm as she advanced my direction. "Vous ne sera pas toucher son!" I knew from his tone this was not going to end well.

Anya's face relaxed into an eerie expression, and she smiled softly at him. She spoke loudly in English, clearly so I would understand. "Very well, Sorin. ..." Now I could tell that her accent was Russian. She looked at me, adding, "I will not touch her." With that, she lashed out at Sorin. The moment her hand made contact with his cheek, my left cheek felt like it was on fire. I yelped as my hand flew to the side of my face in response. His face turned toward me from the force of her blow, and I saw blood streak his cheek. Anya quickly flittered across the street, and Sorin started after her.

I felt a tear fall and started shaking. "Bitch," I said under my breath, hoping she would hear it. I saw a flash of red in the distance—her eyes—and knew she had heard me. I felt pleased about that.

Sorin turned and rushed back to my side. Once he stood next to me, I could see his face up close. She had scratched him, not slapped him. Multiple red lines covered his cheek. I lowered my left hand, expecting to find blood on it, but there was nothing on my palm. I raised my hand to my cheek, again hoping the contact would soothe it.

Sorin moved my hand away, and his cool touch eased the burning sensation in my cheek. "I am so sorry, Mia. Really ... I had no reason to think Anya would seek me out." He looked so worried.

"You're bleeding," was all I could say.

He slipped his sleeve over his fist, swiping it across his cheek. The bleeding had already stopped, and the lines on his cheek were closing before my eyes. He wrapped his free arm around me and pulled me toward the building next to us. Sorin leaned against the wall, silent.

I lay against him, trying not to cry. "Who is she?" I eventually managed. "What did you do to her ... to make her so. ..." There was no question they had a past.

"Anya is young. She is used to getting her way."

I shook my head. "But what did you do to her Sorin?" I was gradually collecting myself and had fought off crying.

"It is not what I did ... it is what I did not do."

I took a step back and looked at him, puzzled.

He crossed his arms and sighed. "As I said, Anya is young ... new to this life. She is used to men falling at her feet. She plays with men of your kind as if they are there simply for her amusement. Two years ago I was in Paris visiting Monique, and she had just taken Anya in. Her sister had turned her ... and then shortly afterward abandoned Anya to travel with a male acquaintance of Monique's. Anya felt her sister had left her behind, and she was very lonely. The pain of separation was fresh with her." I felt no compassion for her, but I continued to listen in silence. "Anya showed ... an interest in me. But I had no desire to ... commit, as you may word it. Monique tried to convince me Anya and I would be a good match. When Monique continued to inject herself, I left. I have not spoken to her since ... that is, until a few days ago. Monique and Anya had no knowledge I already belonged to someone."

I started to fidget, not wanting to stay on the empty sidewalk anymore. I turned and started back to where Sorin had parked.

He caught my hand. "Mia, what about dinner?"

I turned back, flabbergasted he would even suggest it. "Dinner?" It came out high-pitched and strained. "Anya came out of nowhere, threw herself all over you, and ... for a moment I thought you were about to ki—" I stopped my own rambling and changed tacks. "She wanted me dead, Sorin. Not just dead—she was ready to rip out my jugular and leave me to bleed out right on the sidewalk. She wanted to kill me." I raised my voice, and my words came out in a rush. "I saw her fangs, Sorin. ... And when she struck you I felt it."

His face filled with anguish, and he reached for my hand.

I backed away and shook my head. "I have lost any desire to eat ... take me home." A part of me felt bad, but I just wanted to get as far away from there as possible.

He looked at me and then toward the corner. Sorin held the SUV keys out for me to take.

"What?" I asked, not sure what he wanted me to do.

"Take the keys, go wait in the car, and I'll be right back." He took my hand and placed the keys in my palm, pressing my fingers around them.

"Where are you going?" I asked, panicked. I looked in the direction Anya had headed earlier.

Sorin looked at me as the overhead light caught his eyes. I loved it when they looked like that, silvery-blue pools. "Mia," he said, saddened. "Anya is gone ... I promise. Just let me go get you something to eat, please. We will take it home for you to enjoy if you wish."

I could see he wanted to salvage some part of our night out. "Fine … but I'm going with you," I stated, handing his keys back to him.

He wrapped an arm protectively around me as we walked to the corner. The music grew as we turned along the sidewalk, descending the steps leading into the restaurant. He let go of me just inside the entrance and walked to the hostess stand.

A plump Italian-mother type with rosy cheeks smiled at him. "Quante per cena stasera?" She started to reach for menus.

Sorin's back was to me, so I couldn't see his face. His hand reached over the podium and gently laid the menus down. I moved slightly, catching his face in profile. I saw his mouth move slowly, but I couldn't hear the words from where I stood.

The woman's face went blank as she listened to him. She quietly said "si" a couple of times, and then she smiled absentmindedly.

Sorin nodded, reached around to his back pocket, and retrieved a bundle of cash neatly folded in a silver money clip. After separating a few bills from the rest, he pressed them into her hand. She simply stood there for a minute, blinking, and then her smile spread into a goofy grin.

He has made her mind mush, I thought, but thankfully kept from saying it out loud.

He had to nod toward the kitchen in order to get her to finally move. "Il pasto successive nella finestra, si prega," he said, loud enough that I could hear.

I felt a little concerned for her, honestly, and wondered if that was what I looked like when Sorin spoke to me.

He turned and rejoined me by the entrance.

"Impressive," was all I said, my tone sarcastic.

He gave a small smile and put his arm around me. I stood and looked around the restaurant, curious to see what I was refusing to enjoy. The tables were covered in a black velvet fabric. There were gold-trimmed wineglasses and small vases filled with roses on each table. Real vines grew throughout the place, covering pillars that led into the dining area. I hadn't observed much by the time the hostess returned with a large black bag, bearing the restaurant's name in gold letters on the side.

My jaw went lax as she held the bag out me. "Godetevi il vostro pasto, Signorina." It had literally been a few minutes; I couldn't imagine how whatever Sorin had ordered could be ready that quickly.

Sorin took the bag, offering her a smile and a "mille grazie." He took my hand and guided me outside.

I stumbled through the door he held open for me. "This cannot be our food … my food." Once outside, I pressed, "What did you do?"

"I politely asked her to box up the next order that came up." He looked into the bag and then back at me. "Do you like eggplant parmesan?" He held the bag closer, looking in a second time. "If not, there is also linguine and clams." He continued down the sidewalk.

Knowing how much he didn't enjoy the smell of food, I found the gesture of his identifying them touching. Still and all, though. ... "Sorin," I quietly scolded him. "You cannot just walk into a restaurant ... and take someone's meal like that."

He gave my hand a gentle squeeze. "Mia, do not worry about it. I gave her plenty of money. I covered the cost of our meal and the food that we now have. I even gave extra and treated the guests to a bottle of the best wine they had. No one will be perturbed."

I relaxed a little and climbed into my seat after he opened the door for me. He put the bag in the back of the SUV as he walked around to the driver's side. As we pulled away, I looked at the dark brick across the sidewalk, shuddering as we passed the exact spot where Anya had infringed on our evening. Something caught my attention, and I peered through the window. The rose Sorin had tucked behind my ear lay on the sidewalk where we had stood. I lifted my hand to the side of my head, confirming I had lost the rose during the encounter earlier. A lump developed in my throat, and I swallowed, trying to force it away. I lowered my hand to my cheek. It was still a little tender when I pressed it.

Sorin looked my direction, and I let my hand drop to my lap. I turned to stare out the window. We drove in silence, neither of us sure what to say. The vehicle filled with a strong smell of food, and I pushed the button to lower the window.

As the fresh air lessened the aroma of dinner, I lay my head back on the seat.

My mind started to drift as I looked at the night sky. I thought of Anya's fangs, wondering if I would feel the same fear when I saw Sorin's. Was she really gone? My eyes drifted shut, and my mind replayed the exact moment when I'd thought he was going to kiss her. I felt hurt, betrayed. What did "Je ne sera jamais choisir vous" mean? I felt furious and frustrated. *Why didn't I remember more of my French?*

The pain I'd felt when Anya struck Sorin was intense, and I wondered what he must have felt. He had explained that we had a partial bond, that he could feel my pain because a part of him flowed through my veins from the night when he'd saved my then pregnant mother. But he had failed to mention that I would also feel his pain. I was still replaying that particular conversation in my head when we returned to the house. It had slowly sunk in how much my cheek hurt, making me realize how much pain he had to be experiencing if he really did feel mine.

He exited his side of the car, and I headed to the front door while he retrieved the black bag. Once inside, he sat the bag on the marble countertop in the middle of the kitchen. I had smelled it all the way home and wished I could feel hungry again.

Sorin started for a plate from the cupboard, but I stopped him. "That's not necessary … I'm not hungry."

He turned toward me, looking disappointed. I picked up the bag and easily placed the whole thing in the scarcely filled refrigerator. I closed the fridge door and could no longer contain the questions filling my head. "What does 'Je ne sera jamais choisir vous' mean?" I blurted out. I had butchered the French words—my French was even worse than I'd thought— but it sounded close enough.

In an instant, Sorin was sitting across from where I stood. I leaned against the counter behind me, crossing my arms and awaiting the answer. He gazed down at the marble before him, and then locking his eyes with mine, he said, "It means, 'I will never choose you.'"

My heart skipped a beat. "Well … no wonder it enraged Anya." My voice was devoid of any sympathy for her. I motioned to the stove across the kitchen. "I should be thankful I don't own a cute little bunny. We would've come home to bunny soup." I was only trying to lighten the mood. But the expression that covered Sorin's face told me he had absolutely no idea what I was referring to. "Never seen that movie, huh?" I shrugged. "I should know by now that many references are lost on you." I sighed, and my eyes fell to his arms resting on the marble in front of him. A dark stain on his gray sleeve caught my attention. I looked up at his cheek. It held no sign of earlier events. I couldn't help but start to raise my left hand to my cheek as I remembered how it felt. But I caught myself, not wanting to upset him further, and lowered my hand. I quickly started to feel anxious.

Sorin tilted his head slightly. "Anya is gone, Mia. … I promise you, you have nothing to worry about."

He'd said it with total faith, but I didn't feel as confident. "I doubt that, Sorin. She hates me. She wants you for herself … and if she thinks there is a chance with you. …" I paused. "In the end, she is a woman, and she seemed determined."

He slowly shook his head. "She knows now there is no future for her and me."

Feeling argumentative suddenly, I said loudly, "There is always a possibility in a woman's mind."

"Mia. ... She left knowing I had chosen you, "he insisted. My grasp tightened around my own arms. "For now, Anya is hopeful you will lose interest in me. I even realize there is a likelihood of that actual outcome." He shook his head, and his voice rose. "Mia. ... It is no longer a question in my mind that you are my future. After tonight Anya knows it too."

My nails dug into my arms, and my pulse quickened. "There are no guarantees," I shot back. I was not ready to put so much faith into a future with Sorin. I had been shown over and over the uncertainties in life. The world could be cruel.

He pounded a fist into the counter, causing a cracking sound. "There are guarantees for my kind, Mia. ... A guarantee you will forever be a part of someone. Feel someone's love, loss, and everything in between." His eyes pleaded for me to believe him.

I understood what he was getting at. "Yes, I know!" I yelled. "The bond, joining yourself and your partner's blood. You have explained it. But blood must be shared, you said. I understand you gave a part of yourself to me many years ago, before I was even born. You have gone on about how you feel what I do because of that decision. But that alone does not make any kind of future for us a guara—" I froze, and my eyes widened. I pictured Anya again. Recalled how she had leaned into him, smelled him. Then had turned to me with utter disgust. I gasped. She had smelled me on Sorin ... maybe in

Sorin. Had that been what caused the encounter to turn violent? Why he was insisting on Anya's accepting us? I felt my eyes water as tears began to form. I dropped my arms to my sides, digging my nails into my palms. "Tell me!" I screamed, not wanting to believe Sorin had done it.

"Mia ... please calm down." His voice was low.

My hand rose to my cheek. "That's why I felt it," I said, realizing it all made sense now. "How could you?" I forced out quietly as a few tears fell.

Sorin looked at me, his face twisted in shame. "Mia ... just let me explain."

I looked at the floor in front of me, my heart thumping in my chest. I couldn't look at him. The thought of him making this decision that should have been mine tore me up inside. "When?" I demanded.

"You had passed out. I carried you to your room. After feeling you in my arms, smelling you. ... I set you down on the bed, and you reached out to me." He said it all softly.

I lifted my right arm, wiped away a few more tears, and dropped my hand to my neck. I began imagining Sorin's mouth there. I stole a quick glance at his face. Oddly, his eyes were fixed on my left arm.

"I swear ... I stopped myself a moment after I began." His eyes didn't budge, and I looked down at my arm. Turning it slightly I saw the two faintest bruises. Even lighter than they had been the day of the funeral. I had thought they had been made by his fingers. But as he relived that moment of tasting my blood his eyes burned deeper into that specific place on my arm.

I had no doubt now: his fangs had caused the small circles. I wondered what this revelation meant for my future. "So you are trying to excuse it by saying it was only a little you took from me … and while I was passed out, helpless. What about the joining of blood?" I looked back to the floor, knowing any second he would try to make eye contact.

"As I said, Mia … I stopped myself as soon as I began. There is no need to be concerned that a bond has been made between us. The only reason you felt Anya strike me was because your blood was still lingering in my body … and it was rather painful." He sounded sincere and still very upset with himself. "Being alone with you for the first time after all those years of … it was too much for me. Forgive me." He sounded like he was being honest, and I relaxed a little.

There was silence for a few minutes, and then Sorin spoke. "I can leave if you wish." His voice sullen.

The thought of him leaving me pierced my heart. I looked up at him finally. "You would leave me? … Just like that?" I couldn't hide the heartbreak I was unexpectedly feeling. My pain filled my voice.

He weakly smiled. "It would only be for the night, Mia. … I cannot imagine being away from you any longer than necessary. I just thought some time away from me would be appreciated."

I closed my eyes and rubbed my temples, frustrated that I had revealed how the thought of him leaving made me feel. Maybe a night apart would be good for me. I bit the corner of my lip, not wanting to say it out loud. I nodded a yes and left the kitchen. In the doorway, I turned back to steal one last glimpse of him.

Sorin wasn't there. An empty bar stool was all that greeted my gaze.